CW01657713

Twelve Stories *for* Twelve Sections

An anthology of Cornish short fiction
inspired by Cornwall's Protected Landscape

Cornwall
National
Landscape

Twelve Sections

01 Hartland
Giggling in my Jar - Gareth Rees

02 Pentire Point to Widemouth
Survival Tips - Jane Pugh

03 The Camel Estuary
Trading Places - Polly Roberts

04 Carnewas to Stepper Point
The Returners - Annamaria Murphy

05 St Agnes
Perran in the Sands - Emma Timpany

06 Godrevy to Portreath
Little Lights - Clare Howdle

07 West Penwith
The Coffin Path - C.M.Davis

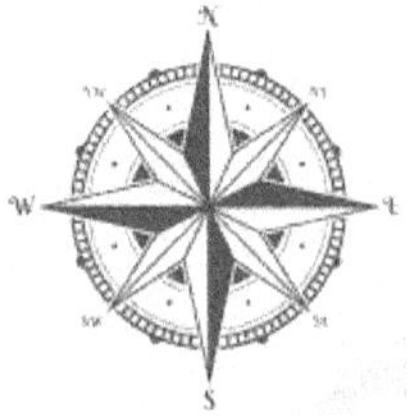

Cornwall National Landscape

08 South Coast Western
Now is the Time for us to Rise from Sleep - Cathy Rentzenbrink

09 South Coast Central
Lone Cypress - Philip Marsden

10 South Coast Eastern
The Incidents - Wyl Menmuir

11 Rame Head
The Black Prince - Edward Rowe

12 Bodmin Moor
The Monkey in the Woodshed - Luke Thompson

Published in Great Britain 2025
Hermitage Press Cornwall.
hermitagepress.co.uk

A CIP catalogue record for this book is
available from the British Library

Cover art and illustrations: James Innerdale
Cover re-design and Typesetting: Sam Stone
Printed and bound by TJ Books, Padstow, Cornwall

ISBN 978-1-7394535-7-2

9 781739 453572 >

CONTENTS

INTRODUCTION

We journey around the sun but never feel it move, yet our personal journeys within the landscape can move us, creating mindful and subliminal connections to our surroundings.

Cornwall National Landscape is a protected landscape, so unique and diverse that it's the only Area of Outstanding Natural Beauty in the United Kingdom with twelve legally designated unique sections comprising one thousand square kilometres of coastline, estuary and moorland.

I am privileged to lead the team and partnership that collaborates to conserve and enhance this living and working landscape. We are united by a common purpose: to make a positive difference, with and for the people, place, nature and climate.

The landscape is our constant companion. Steadfast in its support, it reflects what we're feeling and thinking and, without having to be asked, provides us with what we require to process our emotions, experiences and thoughts. Its elemental qualities shift with the laws of physics and time, of course, but, though it contains both echoes of the past and the promise of the future, it is ever present, it is honest and, if you look hard enough, it contains truth.

Perhaps that's why we seek its company – so that we too can be present and honest with ourselves. It has the power to literally bring us back to earth, providing us with perspective. It comforts, challenges, inspires, teaches and facilitates a natural recalibration of our senses.

In each of the twelve stories in this collection, there is evidence of such a connection to and communication with the landscape. In terms of content and theme, they are, like their settings, distinct, but there's an invisible thread running throughout: a palpable and profound sense of place.

Whether you spend time in nature or not, the connection with it through art and language can be equally powerful and transformative. Storytelling, deeply rooted in both our individual and shared experiences, is part of our cultural heritage. This anthology has been crafted to capture your imagination and guide your own connection and engagement with the landscape. Perhaps it will encourage you to explore the landscape around you and maybe even inspire you to tell stories of your own in the future.

Our *'Art in the Landscape'* initiative, of which this anthology is a part, is designed to enable a diverse range of creative responses to the landscape, from both skilled practitioners and the general public. Cornwall National Landscape is committed to increasing access for all to the protected landscape by creating accessible and inclusive experiences and opportunities designed to allow individuals to connect in a way that interests and inspires them. And we hope you enjoy this redesigned anthology inspired by Cornwall's protected landscape, as much as our previous readers have.

A special thanks must be made to Melodie Manners and Dr Paul Taylor-McCartney, without whose commitment, energy and passion, this project would not have been realised. And without whom the hardback version of this truly Cornish Book would not have won the prestigious *Gorsedh Kernow Holyer an Gof Award* in 2025 for Literary Fiction.

With gratitude, *EJ Browning*
Partnership Manager

Cornwall
National
Landscape

GIGGLING IN MY JAR

by Gareth Rees
(Section 01 - Hartland)

Lifting his biretta, for fear of losing it to gravity's pull, Hawker reaches for the hem of his cassock and feels a twinge in his spine. Standing on the lip of the cliff before his writing hut, his sanctuary, he's desperate to pass water. It's not an easy task at the best of times, but when adorned in the garments of his calling, there's much rummaging and lifting involved in the task. It's August, yet there's a persistent wind, and his stole, a replica of the vestment discovered in St Cuthbert's tomb, whips him.

After several minutes, Hawker manages to lift both the cassock and the surplice he wears over it, and feeling the breeze on him, he sighs, delighted to be free and wild, just as he was in boyhood. Imagine if he were seen!

But this exuberance is brief, for though he once discharged 'rivers of living water', to (mis)use the Saviour's words, now nought but a feeble trickle issues from him, and that with a distressing lack of urgency.

Hawker looks to the Atlantic. Despite the season, it's frothing and furious under a leaden firmament that obscures the view of Wales often visible with skies swept clean of cloud, and he swears it ululates at his infirmity. Seagulls riot and shriek. Hawker has made a habit of talking to birds, as his beloved St Cuthbert did before him. But believing gulls to be possessed of the souls of dead sailors who have not been granted a comfortable final resting place, he feels a deep unease and is struck dumb in their presence.

Hawker has spent a lifetime gathering the sea's grim harvest, pulling lifeless forms from the surf and, back bent, their dead weight across his shoulders, carrying them up the cliff path to St Morwenna's churchyard and giving them a Christian burial. Every man's right. But these avian vessels hold the souls Hawker could not save, and their shrill cries of injustice fill his skull like a migraine. One of these unfortunate gulls lands on the cliff edge, not a yard from where Hawker stands, and leers at him. The red tip of its beak reminds Hawker of rouged lips. It's a comical image, but there's also something sinister and unsettling about it.

These thoughts of the dead bring to mind Hawker's late wife, his dear Charlotte. Hawker always thought that

Charlotte offered him the tenderness he had longed for from childhood, that her quiet strength and steadfast support had kept him tethered to this earth, allowing him to discharge his duties and pursue his purpose to the best of his abilities. But since she left him, he has realised that it was she who had lifted him up, allowed him to touch the heavens. She brought him lightness. She brought him peace.

Though he nursed Charlotte through her illness, imploring his Lord to spare her, he could not save her. And his grief at her passing was relentless, a great black wave that overwhelmed him, forcing him to seek solace in the bouts of oblivion offered by the opium pipe.

Now, although he's rediscovered happiness with Pauline and become a father to their three girls, he feels a weight pressing down on his chest, as if it were him who had been buried beneath a flagstone at St Morwenna. Feeling a powerful urge to return to his church, to visit Charlotte, he attempts to step back from the cliff edge – but he cannot. Something keeps him rooted, between the safety of his writing hut – built of driftwood, earth and the sweat of his brow, a place he could be with God – and the abyss, with nothing but the damned seabirds and the incessant waves for company.

It's now, for the first time, that he considers how he came to be here, and why he's dressed for church. Where are his well-worn fisherman's boots and jersey and his claret tailcoat?

But Plymouth —

Hawker was unwell at Penally, the home of his brother, Claude. And Pauline, their girls and he departed Boscastle for Plymouth, where he was born, in search of medical advice. He did not wish it. Nevertheless, there he went, at Pauline's insistence. They took a house on Lockyer Street, where he rallied somewhat and they readied themselves to set off once more, this time for Morwenstow and home.

But they didn't leave. Instead, Hawker decided to be photographed.

He had been 'taken' on only two previous occasions. Both times by Mr Thorn of Bude Haven. Firstly at Morwenstow and latterly at Bude with Pauline and their girls. Dear, dear things. Hawker took no pleasure in the fearsome ritual, dreading the alchemy of the black box, the mysteries within it, but he couldn't deny it, he wanted to be remembered. Else what had it all been for?

And so, Pauline helped him into his vestments – Morwenna, Rosalina and Juliot fussing and yapping about him like pups eager to run free and terrorise the local wildlife – and in the sunlight of an August morning, he had set off for George Street and the studio of Mr John Hawke, a man who all had assured him was fit for a task of such profound import.

For some time, even before death had placed its heavy hand on his shoulder, Hawker had felt anxious about the end. Not death itself, for he was as eager as any Christian to enter the Kingdom. But abandoning Pauline and the girls. There was no coin, no land or property, no wealth to speak of. But heading for George Street, he felt as carefree as he had as a bachelor at Oxford.

It was a long walk, taking him down Union Street and Devonport Hill, but his 'cup runneth over' with life, and he stopped to tip his biretta to passers-by enlivened by the sight of a vicar dressed for the pulpit strolling their common path, and even to banter with a pair of rooks bickering in the long grass. 'You behave yourselves now, lads. Our Lord has his eyes on you, as he does on each of us.'

It took Hawker more than half an hour to reach his destination, where a sign over the door read 'Mr John Hawke Esq. Photographer's Studio', printed in a bold serif font on a black background. A black curtain had been pulled across the window, obscuring the interior. Hawker scoffed. The place had the look of a funeral parlour.

As he reached for the brass doorknob, Hawker heard a soft thud and then became aware of a commotion at his feet. Looking down, he saw a jackdaw. Distressed, the bird flapped its wings in wild bursts, in a pathetic attempt to take to the skies, but its legs were mangled.

'My dear fellow,' said Hawker, bending down and scooping up the injured bird.

Startled, like a mackerel on a hook, it attempted to flap its wings, but Hawker held it tight, and it soon became still. It eyed him, its pupils rolling in their whites.

Hawker massaged the silver necklace below the bird's head with his thumbs, an action that appeared to induce calm. 'Thrice happy bird! No longer,' he said, recalling a line from Cowper.

Holding the jackdaw to his chest with one hand, Hawker turned the doorknob.

Upon entering the studio, a bell over the doorway jangled and a boy appeared.

'I have a bird, lad,' said Hawker. 'It's hurt. It needs help.'

Grasping the fabric of his short trousers and shuffling his feet, as though he needed to visit the water closet, the boy stared at Hawker, tears forming in his eyes. Hawker recognised this as the look of love – not romantic love, of course, but the love the Lord demands we have for our fellow man, a feeling of the deepest care and compassion.

It seemed absurd, but Hawker also sensed this child was offering absolution for his failings, and he felt the lifting of responsibility, both for his life and for the lives of others.

The boy's skin was soft and so white it glowed. This pale angel didn't speak, but he held out his hands, and Hawker, mesmerised, handed the jackdaw into his care without further comment or question.

The boy regarded the broken bird with the look of a parent nursing a sick child. Hawker experienced a surge of pure love, the like of which he had only felt before following the birth of his own children.

Hawke, tall and thin, emerged, breaking the spell the boy had cast.

'Reverend Hawker.'

'Mr Hawke.'

'Go now, Philip.' Hawke did not look at the boy, but Hawker sensed he cared deeply for him.

Philip left the studio.

'Quiet lad.'

'My son is mute, Reverend.'

'I'm sorry.'

'There's nothing to be sorry for, Reverend. Philip's as bright as a new penny, and he doesn't require words.'

Hawker nodded and smiled. 'I've charged your Philip with the task of caring for an injured bird, Mr Hawke. A jackdaw I discovered in the road. I trust it won't prove too much of a burden.'

'No, Reverend. Not at all. My wife was a kindly soul, and Philip has much of his mother in him.' Hawke possessed a stern countenance, but his voice could have soothed the most distraught infant.

'I'm sorry for your loss, Mr Hawke. I pray it wasn't recent.'

'My wife died in childbirth, Reverend,' said Hawke, briefly turning his head to break eye contact with Hawker.

'My wife, my first wife, and I were never blessed with children, but the loss of her is a wound that will never heal.'

Hawke exhaled. The two bereaved men shared a moment of silent reflection.

It was Hawker who disturbed this communal remembering. 'Right, then. Where would you like me?'

'If you could take a seat, Reverend,' said Hawke, refocused on his business, as though the talk of loss had never taken place. 'I won't be a minute.'

Left alone in the studio for the first time, Hawker surveyed the space. It was almost dark, a chink in the curtain permitting no more than a narrow beam of sunlight – but there wasn't much to see anyway. Bare boards and whitewashed walls. A black screen had been set up behind a low platform, on which had been positioned a carved mahogany chair with a high back and a seat of red leather.

Hawker sat in the chair, and a moment later Mr Hawke returned, carrying his camera, a black box with a brass lens, affixed to a tripod. Hawker imagined a medieval executioner advancing to the scaffold with his axe, and a mild nausea lapped at his insides.

Hawker did not speak for several minutes, Hawker shifting anxiously in the chair while the photographer arranged his contraption before him, its thin wooden legs clacking on the boards each time Hawke fidgeted with it.

Dressed in a black suit, Hawke could have been mistaken for an undertaker and, Hawker noted, looked just about ready for the grave. Though he was a youngish man, he was frail and his skin was as pale as his son's. A monochrome man, apart from his hair, which was as red as clay.

'Right, Reverend,' said Hawke, taking hold of the curtain, and tugging it across the rail. 'Let there be light.'

Expecting an explosion of sunlight, Hawker squinted. But no such explosion occurred. The room did brighten, but the light was milky, like weak tea. Hawker reasoned that Hawke must have applied a treatment to the glass.

For what purpose, he didn't know. To him, the new art of photography resided in the dark realm of alchemy. It was a medium Dee would no doubt have embraced.

'I need you to be on your best behaviour now, Reverend.'

'I'm your servant, Mr Hawke.'

'Still as a statue.'

The photographer stooped and vanished beneath a black sheet to peer through his little hole. It caused Hawker not inconsiderable anxiety that he could not see what the photographer saw, and he shuffled in the chair.

'Still,' repeated Hawke, the command firm but his tone still gentle. 'As a statue.'

Hawker was about to offer his apologies when the photographer held up his index finger in the manner of a parent silently shushing an unruly child.

Hawker's anxiety increased with each moment Hawke spent huddled beneath his wrinkled shroud, seeing what Hawker could not see. Seeing Hawker.

Suddenly the photographer lifted his arms, and the sheet spread wide like the wings of a raven, before just as suddenly drooping over his back like a cloth thrown over a table. His right arm emerged, and he gripped the brass cap on the lens between his forefinger and his thumb.

Hawker shifted in his seat again and attempted to assume the countenance of a great and serious man. What Hawker would Hawke capture?

'Still now, Reverend.'

'As a statue,' said Hawker.

There was a flash, as the sun finally burst through the glass. Hawke's hair was alight, transforming in the sunlight from ochre to an orange blaze. Hawker was in awe, but it was an awe accompanied by fear. Not the fear one feels when threatened with harm, but that which one experiences when standing on the edge of a cliff looking out over the water beholding a fierce sunrise. Or the fear St Francis must have felt as he received the gift of the stigmata. Perhaps it was not fear at all but freedom. Salvation.

Hawker admonished himself for allowing his mind to get the better of him. Nevertheless, it's a fearsome thing to be created by another, and he began to wish he had allowed a multitude of Hawkers – a multitude of selves – to be produced. Too late now. He will leave behind so few imitations from which the living will attempt to deduce his character, his true nature. With Hawker's perishing, all that will remain besides photographs is memories, which will fade, unless committed to print or spoken to future generations, passed down, in altered form, to be distorted and embellished.

Hawker saw the photographer's hand move, his fingers tighten on the lens cap – and his body was granite.

Hawke removed the lens cap. Hawker stared at the glass. Stared and stared and stared.

'Still.'

And Hawker was still, as he was created anew, not by God but by Mr John Hawke, photographer, stranger.

Reborn but also fixed in time, rigid as a corpse.

In this moment, as he was trapped in the black box, Hawker thought of Charlotte. And he felt guilty for thinking of the dead and not the living.

'Finished,' said Hawke, replacing the lens cap, shrugging off the sheet and lifting his contraption.

'How long?'

'You will have it in a few minutes, Reverend.' Hawke left.

Hawker slumped into the seat and closed his eyes, but before he had allowed himself a deep breath, he felt a tap on his leg.

It was the boy, Philip. His arms were outstretched, his palms held up as if waiting to receive the sacrament. But resting in those palms was not the bread symbolising the broken body of Christ but the broken body of the jackdaw.

It was dead.

Standing up and lifting the bird from the boy's palms and placing it on the chair, Hawker recalled a line from Barham. 'The Jackdaw sat on the Cardinal's chair!' He smiled though he felt a profound sadness. Turning to the boy, he saw that his eyes, the deep green of seaweed, were drowned in tears.

A moment later, Hawke re-emerged and handed Hawker the photograph.

'My apologies,' Hawker said. 'For the bird.'

Hawke glanced at the dead jackdaw. 'I hope you are satisfied with the photograph, Reverend. I believe it's a good likeness.'

Hawker nodded. 'Thank you, Mr Hawke. Please send your bill to Morwenstow.' And then, as he left, 'Goodbye, Philip.'

Hawker didn't return immediately to Lockyer Street but instead took a detour and visited St Mary & St Boniface's Cathedral, where he and Pauline had attended benediction the previous Sunday. It was there, seated in the rear pew, he realised he still held the photograph in his hand. He opened the folded card that encased it and beheld himself. A vicar of the Church of England, a good and great man, the humility in his eyes softening his austere countenance. But the keen eye would see that the right hand clutched the arm of the chair, while the left hand was curled into a claw. For in the moment the image had been captured, a pain had spread through Hawker's arms. A pain that alerted him to his fate, even if he didn't recognise it at the time.

Leaving the cathedral, Hawker no longer cared about his legacy. He was prepared to leave life to the living, to join the dead, to be judged by his Lord, whose right it is to pass judgement on his children.

But, but Ford Park Cemetery —

Hawker doesn't float, as a ghost might float, but there is a lightness to his movement, as though he's held up on strings like a marionette, and he feels a sense of joyous anticipation. There's something to see, something important, something dependent on his attendance.

To his left, as he progresses up the path between the gravestones, he sees the tower of St Mary & St Boniface's Cathedral, where he looked upon the photograph. It feels like a moment in somebody else's life. It means nothing to him.

He feels disconnected from the physical realm, but the life still burns within him. There is no thought of the past, or of the future – and his soul grows lighter still.

But now, having seen a huddle of mourners in the long grass of the non-conformist plot, he slows. He's confused. It's not as he had expected. Did he not give his life to the Church of England?

He sees the mourners from above now, from the bird's view. They are all dressed in claret to honour the dead man, who was fond of that colour.

A woman. Still young. A mother. And her three children. It's Pauline and their girls – and his confusion is submerged in sorrow. He will miss these dear souls a dreadful measure.

He observes from a distance now, high above this Catholic funeral, and he questions if it is, after all, Hawker's mortal remains that reside within the coffin resting in the blackness.

But there are no answers. We suffer even as we ascend. Nevertheless, Hawker is certain there will be light.

And then he is back atop the cliff.

The seagulls still cry below, but their noise no longer concerns him, for he is finished with life. The gull with the rouged lips returns. It looks at him with one eye, and then it winks. He is sure of it. It winks!

He's no longer anchored. He's able to step back from the edge of the cliff, and he turns and begins the walk back to his church. To St Morwenna. He feels light. He is light. Apart from a heaviness in his hand. A presence holding it, guiding him.

Jackdaws, that 'great frequenter of the church' – Cowper again! – caw to their life mates.

He stands above the burial place below the pulpit.

'HERE LIES THE BODY OF CHARLOTTE HAWKER. FOR NEARLY FORTY YEARS THE WIFE OF ONE OF THE VICARS OF THIS CHURCH.'

He is home. And he laughs like a child.

But, but, but —

Seagulls riot and shriek. Hawker has made a habit of talking to birds, as his beloved St Cuthbert did before him.

AUTHOR

Gareth Rees

I dream of a remote place where I could write undisturbed. A place like Saint Govan's cliffside cell in Pembrokeshire, Wales, the land of my ancestors. Reverend R S Hawker, the opium smoking Victorian clergyman-poet who inspired *'Giggling in my jar'*, built himself a place like this in Cornwall, my adopted home. Hawker's Hut, the National Trust's smallest property, sits on the North Cornwall coast, near Higher Sharpnose Point. Built into the cliffside, it's a tall man's stride from a sheer drop to Cotton Beach, where Hawker collected driftwood for its construction, as well as the corpses of drowned sailors. It looks out over the often moody Atlantic. As soon as I read Sabine Baring-Gould's biography of Hawker, I knew I was going to attempt to bring this famous 'eccentric' back to life (sort of) on the page. But it wasn't until I walked from Hawker's church, St Morwenna, in Morwenstow – where I discovered the final resting place of Hawker's first wife, Charlotte, just below the pulpit where the great

man delivered his sermons
– to Hawker's Hut that I saw both the start and the end of his, and my, story. I sat in Hawker's sanctuary, listening to the waves breaking and the seagulls – possessed by the souls of the long dead sailors Hawker couldn't offer a Christian burial – lamenting their fate, and assembled the bones of it.

*There's no direct reference to the phrase *'giggling in my jar'* in the narrative. It comes from Camera Lucida by Roland Barthes, which was one of the primary inspirations for the story: "*What I want, in short, is that my (mobile) image, buffeted among a thousand shifting photographs, altering with situation and age, should always coincide with my (profound) 'self'; but it is the contrary that must be said: 'myself' never coincides with my image; for it is the image which is heavy, motionless, stubborn (which is why society sustains it), and 'myself' which is light, divided, dispersed; like a bottle-imp, 'myself' doesn't hold still, giggling in my jar...*"

SURVIVAL TIPS

by Jane Pugh

(Section 02 - Pentire Point to Widemouth)

Homeless Guy warned me, said. 'Use sun cream, wear a hat, avoid sun stroke. Sun stroke makes you sick and tired.' I am sick and tired. I want you to know I love you. You're the best thing that ever happened to me, even if me and your mum aren't together anymore because she went off with Gavin. Our dentist.

Son, little lad, I'm being honest and I've got to tell you I'm seriously thinking of doing myself in. Sorry. I've reached St Nectan's Glen. The shade from the trees is nice. We've been before. Remember paddling? Your little toes in the water. Brave. I'm not brave. I've got my trainers and socks on. I won't take them off, I won't. The water is cool, I'd feel better for it, but I can't. Crying now.

Homeless Guy said the water at the Glen is clean enough to drink but he's ex-military and lives in a tent over Delabole. Hard as. It's windy up there – no shelter and the skies are crazy wide – but he prefers it. 'Freedom sky' he calls it. If he said the water was gin and tonic, now we're talking. That's my preferred tipple with my friends after work. I say, 'Don't put too much ice in it, you'll drown it.' Gin's become a bit of a favourite with me, but I'll drink anything I can get my hands on since the fire that killed my best friend and his girlfriend, who I actually fancied. She was sweet and clever. Not that I'd have done anything, I love your mum. I got out of the burning barn, they didn't. The local paper said I '… walked away, unscathed.'

It's pretty here.

I told Homeless Guy I was considering ending it all and he said, 'Been there, mate.' I thought he'd try and talk me out of it, but he didn't. Instead, he said, if I was up for it, he'd give me a mission to go on a walk and he'd help me with some survival tips. He asked if I'd ever been in the army or the Scouts or anything like that. I laughed, I said 'I'm an estate agent. My survival plan is getting a 20 per cent discount dry cleaning my Paul Smith suit.' He'd never heard of Paul Smith. I said, 'Oh, you ignoramus!' and he laughed.

One more walk. My aim is to start here, at the Glen, get myself to Boscastle, then walk along the cliffs to Tintagel and jump off the bridge in front of a thousand tourists. Or if I decide to live, I'll get myself a very nice dinner at

Rock. I'm a vegetarian, but I'm going to have a steak. In fact, I'll get two steaks, one for me and one for Homeless Guy. I'll take it back to Delabole, up on the wide, sweeping farmland and he can eat it in his tent, we could warm it through on his camping stove, or, if he prefers, he could have it cold.

Homeless Guy said, 'If you do it, can I have your car?' I rolled my eyes. It's a classic Saab. I'm old school. Yes, RnB is okay but, if you want the truth, I like Soul, I saw Lionel Ritchie at the Eden Project. What a dude. Smooth.

He can have my car even though he won't tell me his name. I told him, 'I'm Craig' when we first met and shook hands. His were rough and coarse. Like the North Cornwall landscape. He had beautiful hands.

When I was a boy, me and Mum came to the Glen over and over. Out of the lashing wind and sea, amongst the trees, we'd stare, mesmerised by the stream. Everything all around is green. I mean, like, a hundred different types of green. The leaves, the trees, the moss, the ferns.

The water is green, too, and noisy and alive. Bubbling and battling. Everything here is alive. Everything.

That's nice, isn't it? Shame I want to die. Shame the rage and fear has got the better of me. Shame I feel lost. Shame life has no meaning. Shame I can't hold on anymore.

Homeless Guy told me to drink the water from the Glen. Survival tip number one, stay hydrated. Get to the Glen and drink the water. Son, you're not allowed to copy this. Under any circumstances. You're only four years old, your system isn't strong enough and your mum would kill me.

I drink the water. I lie down flat on the bank and scoop up the water in my hand. One, two, three big gulps. The ground is muddy and now, so am I. Which is seriously not cool. I'm wearing my casuals but still.

The water feels nice in my tummy and has cooled my brain. Maybe I will paddle…

I walk down the road to Boscastle, and as I walk, I apply more sun cream to my neck and my nose. I might be thinking about offing myself, but I care about what I look like. I see a man, my age, mid-twenties, having a pee and a fag and wearing a turban. Is 'turban' the right word? If I live, I'll google it and find out. He's parked his black, electric SUV in the lay-by and Bhangra music blasts out. His girlfriend and his mates are in the car, laughing at him. There is the hedgerow and the field and the sea beyond, which is wide and endless and fluffy. As I pass, he says, 'It's brilliant in the countryside, you can pee anywhere.' I'd never thought of that. Being Cornish, I've taken it for granted that the whole landscape is your en suite. They're down from Wembley, first time in Cornwall and happy. Good luck to them.

As he pissed, he just stared at the sea, trying to understand it but accepting he couldn't.

I think it's hard to accept the un-understandable. I can't. We were doing up the vintage tractor in the barn, late at night. Battery on charge. Relaxing after with a drink, fell asleep. Fire. Smoke like oil. Stupid. Pointless.

I walk on, wanting to cry again. Son, there's nothing wrong with crying. Let your tears flow down your heart-shaped face and onto your dinosaur T-shirt.

I bet they've got a wide range of restaurants in Wembley and some decent clubs.

At Boscastle. Homeless Guy had said, 'On your journey find something to eat, trap it, kill it and cook it.' So, I have a vegetarian sausage sandwich at the Toby Jug Cafe. With a salad garnish. And a coke. I'm trying not to drink. Drinking is like the tide coming in and out and it won't stop. Your mum hated it. Here, now, the tide is out and fishing boats, painted PW for Padstow, loll on the flat. I can't see any fishermen. Where do they go when they're onshore? Doing up the spare bedroom? Having a pint at the Wellington Hotel where the girl with the pink hair works?

After lunch (I left a big tip because the staff are well friendly) I walk on the mud-sand towards a bright blue and red fishing boat and my trainers and socks get wet. FFS. I know I shouldn't wear white trainers. I bought you some, do you remember your mum kicking off? 'White trainers round here, what are you thinking?' I like white trainers, Tinie Tempah wears them, what does she know? Homeless Guy said, 'Keep clean, tidy, warm and dry at all times.' How, exactly?

I place my hand on the bow of the fishing boat and I smell fish and salt and mud and sand and I hear seagulls cry, and in the distance, beyond the harbour, the sea gently roaring. Murmuring from the visitors. An old man pushes another old man in his wheelchair towards the kiosk and they order themselves the biggest ice-cream cones known to humankind.

I don't know anything about fishermen, I don't know what they catch, kill and sell. I've no clue. Mum is angry with me because I'm an estate agent and she doesn't want me selling to second-homers. So, I do my very best not to, but the commission is hard to resist. Sorry about that. Sorry about everything. I don't want to be an absent dad because I've no clue who mine is. When I was little I imagined he was a fisherman lost at sea. Your mum went off with our dentist because I've been sad for too long, and I don't blame her. My boss keeps glaring at me because my sales are down. Get off my back. Friends invite me out, but I don't go anymore, and I tried to have sex with the girl with the pink hair from the Wellington, but I couldn't, and she was nice about it, which made it worse.

Son, did you know we live in an Area of Outstanding Natural Beauty? But it's ugly to me. Hard and cruel. Look at the sea and the rock, up against each other. Permanently. Can we not find peace?

Burning and wailing filled the air. And it was too quick and too late to save them and I had to face their families at their funerals. They said they were relieved I'd survived but they hated me really and I hated me really. There are bold, strong churches round here, up on hill tops. Standing the test of time. We don't, do we?

Mum is a dairy farmer, and she knows about life and death. She can kill a chicken with one hard twist. Blimey. No wonder I'm vegetarian. If I make it to Rock, I've changed my mind, I'm going to see what vegetarian specials they've got.

Mum raised me on her own. You were premature and breathed into a machine. Little chest pumping furiously. The fishermen face the sea and Homeless Guy lives in a tent. The man from Wembley has an SUV – electric – that's fifty grand's worth of car. I am not a man.

I'm not a woman either – and they can be stronger, can't they? I'm not strong. We live in North Cornwall, which is mighty and epic, but for three years I've been small and scared. Who needs a weak dad? I didn't and neither do you.

So, where do I go from here?

Tintagel. Homeless Guy said, 'Find shelter.' Here I am at the castle, there's some brilliant knick-knacks in the shop. During lockdown I watched all those 'knights of old' dramas on Netflix, and when I was ten, I loved Merlin on the telly, who kept promising to lay down his life for Arthur and the general good.

When Homeless Guy described shelter, he said it must be secure against the elements. Tintagel Castle lasted ten years before the sea, the rain, the salt and the wind knackered it. Honestly, if you plonked a static caravan on the edge of Pentire Point, it would last longer. Richard, thirteenth-century dreamer, more money than sense, galvanised a work force, more stick than carrot, and built himself a castle where Arthur once looked out to sea. Homeless Guy is a realist and Richard was a dreamer. I'm with Homeless Guy. Where do dreams get you? Nowhere. And I'm not talking about myself since the fire. The tragedy. I've never been a dreamer. How do you get yourself a house in Cornwall? Work your tits off in a job that pays well, that's how. Son, remember that, but I want you to know, I've made a will, everything I've got goes to you so, if it is curtains today, it's all yours. Apart from the Saab, obviously, because Homeless Guy's bagged that.

Homeless Guy says everyone has a choice. Girl with the pink hair, a degree, tattoos and short shorts says the same. Mum always says it too. Have I got a choice? Should I live or die today? Leon didn't have a choice. He died in the fire. Billy didn't have a choice; she died too. But I can decide. Do I jump or have a nice dinner in Rock, at a freshly laid table and a view of the seashore?

Son, I did it. Well, I didn't do it, obviously because here I am, apologising again. I'll avoid too much detail, but I overdosed in the disabled loo back in Tintagel village. I was rescued by a German coach driver. It's very diverse in North Cornwall, you meet people from all over the world. Anyway, I've ruined my socks and trainers in seawater, got mud on my shorts from the Glen and dried vomit from my overdose down a T-shirt your mum gave me.

All things considered, it's been a challenging day.

Later, I saw Homeless Guy and told him he'd have to

wait to inherit the Saab. The wind was up, and the canvas flapped as we sat, knees to knees, in the closeness of his tent. He squeezed my shoulder. We laughed with relief, we felt dizzy almost, like the flittering wind and air, liveable, breathable air. No dinner in Rock, instead, he cooked me local vegetables and pasta. Very nice. 'Cheers!' he said, and we clinked our mugs of tea. Three sugars.

The next day, when I came to see him, he was gone. He was like the father I never had, but I'll be a father to you from now on, I promise. Till the day I die. I mean proper die, in an old people's home, with Sky Sports on the television and the sound of the sea.

On my final walk I saw dozens of thrifts clinging to the cliffs, pink and cheerful like lollipops. I have to say they're my favourite flower. When I fetch you on Thursday, shall we have a look? We can take photos of them on my phone. I know you'll grow up to have regrets as well as happiness, but if I can give you one survival tip, when we're out, exploring life, don't wear your white trainers. It pains me to admit it, but your mum was right about that, my son.

I place my hand on the bow of the fishing boat and I smell fish and salt and mud and sand and I hear seagulls cry, and in the distance, beyond the harbour, the sea gently roaring. Murmuring from the visitors. An old man pushes another old man in his wheelchair towards the ice-cream kiosk.

AUTHOR

Jane Pugh

A vital journey, that's what I chose to write about, because I'd explored North Cornwall for the first time since moving to Penzance twenty-three years ago. I didn't know St. Nectan's Glen and I'd never been to Boscastle. What an oversight! My loss. But now, thanks to the commission, my gain.

It's an Area of Oustanding Natural Beauty – but is it beautiful? Or is it more profound than beauty? I believe it is. It's elemental, bold, powerful, extreme. You know those places that don't care whether there's human existence or not? That's what struck me about North Cornwall. And there's something liberating about that, something honest.

Author photograph: Steve Tanner

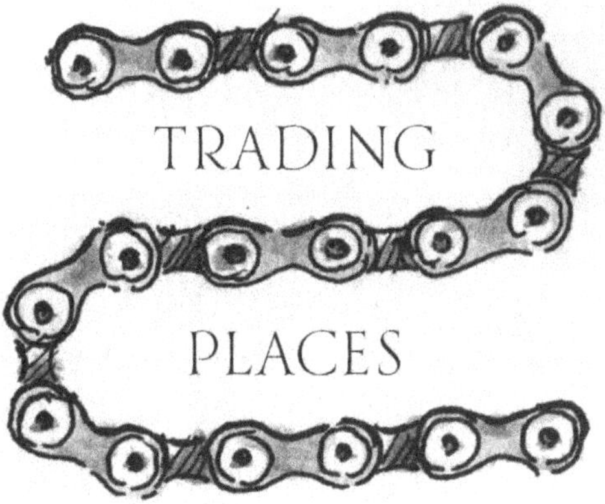

TRADING PLACES

by Polly Roberts

(Section 03 - The Camel Estuary)

When I had first suggested to Maria she might come home with me to Padstow, meet my mum and see where I'd grown up, we were curled around one another on the sofa in her Lisbon apartment, wrapped only in a white sheet. The winter sun had poured in through the window, warming areas of exposed skin, and Maria had said, 'Okay, but only if we wait until your British sun comes out.' We had booked the flight for the coming spring and not spoken more of it.

Spring arrived and so did my nerves. I had moved to Portugal eighteen months earlier, having found a job teaching English at a small academy in central Lisbon. My aim had been to get away from impossibly high prices, low job opportunities, and small-town life. I met Maria at a bar where she sang Fado for tourists like me, and I hadn't thought about home since. Home now was this majestic city built on a hill with sea to dictate direction, delicious food, great wine, and the taste of Maria's lips.

The week before our flight I surprised Maria at her usual gig in the bar Terra Estrela. The room was packed with tiny tables that wobbled on the tiles and populated by English-speaking couples. I ordered a glass of vinho verde and took the last stool at the bar. Maria was dressed in her Fado attire, a long floral dress and a black lacy shawl; I could feel the crowd fall in love just as I had all those months ago.

'Ellie, where is my wine?' was her post-performance demand as she joined me at the bar, planting a lipsticked kiss on my cheek.

'Uma garrafa.' I gestured to the barman, pointing at my glass.

'A bottle? What are we celebrating?' asked Maria.

'Our life in this wonderful city,' I said, passing a twenty euro note across the counter.

'Wonderful to you,' said Maria. 'You earn an English wage and live in a beautiful part of the city.' It was an argument had many times over. 'Here I am selling my culture to your people for a pittance.' She pronounced her words with a force shaped by her beautiful strong jaw, which only made me want to kiss her more. 'One of these days I will have to move back to my grandparents' village,' she said, and I shivered at the prospect of no more Lisboa, no more Maria.

'You are preaching to the converted,' I said. 'I left my home for the same reasons don't forget.'

'Ah yes, and I am happy for it.' Maria moved her mouth to my ear and the argument ended there.

We caught the plane to Bristol in glorious sunshine with a forecast of light rain upon landing. A flight, train, and a bus ride later, and we were sat around Mum's kitchen table, with Maria and her deep in conversation while I struggled to remember what Cornish me was like. Mum was the same as always – round-faced, warm and chatty – and I wondered whether she'd be this way in Lisbon also.

Maria and I walked around Padstow town and I scoffed, 'Everything is for tourists.' It was only spring, and the harbour was already filled with stressed families, drunk lads and rich couples carrying shopping bags.

'Ellie, you are so miserable,' said Maria, 'look how cute it is – all these cottages and cobbled paths.' She insisted we take every side street and wind up and down the maze of roads pulling us from sea to sky and back again. 'It is like we are in a Shakespeare play,' Maria said, to which I tried to explain how her eras were all mixed up, then stopped when I noticed her eyes wince. While I saw the inevitable fudge shops, pasties, jewellery and ice-cream, she saw an idyllic English port-town.

There was an irony we tried to wrap our heads around at night over bad English-supermarket wine and Mum's casserole – I loved Lisbon for its genuine cultural feel, and she felt the same about Padstow, while each of us as locals only saw how disingenuous they were to their past selves.

By day three, Maria's enthusiasm was grating against my angst. Mum had told me her landlord was considering switching to short-term lets, and the worry of this led me to stare at my feet rather than Maria or her delighted observations. 'Stop ruining my holiday,' Maria pulled my hair as we sat watching the ferry to Rock depart for the fifth time that day. She reminded me how she'd put up with my gushing about Lisbon, so the least I could do was let her do the same. 'Remember, you are a tourist in Lisbon, just like these people here. I could blame you for making my home city unaffordable, but I don't.' I bit my tongue before I reminded her of the zillion times she had.

That night she decided on a trip for us, poring over a map my mum had dug out. She'd eyed two ancient bicycles in the garden and announced we were taking a cycling tour. Even on my turf Maria took charge. 'We will take the bikes on the ferry to Rock,' she said with bright eyes, 'then cycle to Wadebridge, sleep at a traditional English B&B, and cycle back along this trail.' She ran her fingers along the Camel Trail running from Wadebridge to Padstow. It was decided, I would holiday at home.

We packed some stuff in Mum's old panniers and left the next morning on the first boat, blessed by sunshine. The tide was in, and I watched the mysterious yellow patches in the water that hinted at what lay beneath. I had forgotten how this was the place where land disappeared and reappeared. At low tide hidden islands revealed themselves, sand banks straddling the middle of the river with no rhyme or reason as to why in one place and not another.

At first, Maria was disappointed by Rock – she had romanticised, from across the river, an ancient fishing village – but she clung to the small row of granite cottages just off the boat and this quenched her dream. I didn't dare remind her of the tonnes of untouched fishing villages in Portugal that she had no interest in, like her grandparent's village, which she threatened to escape to, as if this would be the worst case ever.

We passed the huge, glass-fronted holiday homes, and I averted my gaze, instead focusing on the views of bright green hills above the sparkling, crystalline water. There were white strips of sandy beach and lightly wooded hills to climb at the back. Padstow looked ordinary on the other side, but this new angle left me gawking at my home – a generous, wide river with pristine beaches and wild cliffs leading to the sea, green fields and blue skies, palm and oak trees, surf shops and fishing boats.

We bought a smoothie and ice-cream to share from the surf café and Maria struck up a conversation with the surfer babe serving us, unsubtly eyeing her up as she did. 'Ellie, the Cornish dream is real!' she exclaimed as we left to sit on a bench and slurp our goods. 'Women here are brave and beautiful.' I shrugged, struck by a silent curiosity that I thought the same of Portuguese women. We watched the sail boats and dinghies bob by colourful buoys in the water, and I pondered whether if I were Maria, I would have left Lisbon just as I'd left here – despite all its beauty.

We cycled our bikes along the seafront and left them leaning against the carpark fence as we climbed the sand dune at the back of Rock beach. Doom Bar was as magnificent as I had remembered – people fishing off one end and walking across the middle like there was no sea on either side. The sea was so vast – the mouth cornered by two headlands but only water beyond. 'Why are these sand dunes here?' asked Maria, and we both wondered, each as stumped as the other, how such giant sandcastles could be built here and nowhere else, drawn upward by some unknown, localised force.

After a picnic lunch of Cornish Yarg sandwiches, of which I savoured every bite, we reclaimed our bikes and took the back roads down to Porthilly, then along to Dinham Farm Caravan Park, before re-joining the B-road to Wadebridge. The route gave a new perspective of the river – long, wide, and laid bare for us to see. We marvelled at the white sandy patches of the Bar and turquoise blue of the water, the muddy sides like the glistening backs of whales. The decline downward ran through a patchwork of fields, brown with freshly turned soil. I'd never taken these roads before and was struck by the quaint stone-cottaged hamlets and tucked-away feel. Discovering new civilisation hidden behind familiar hedges felt uncanny.

Maria kept complaining, 'I can't see anything,' hitting her hand against the edge of the hawthorn and hazel as she cycled on, but I told her how the hedges made the view all the more magical when it arrived. At the next opening between dense green, we both stood, straddling our bikes with mouths open in disbelief. All along, smothered behind them, had been an expansive view of hills in varying shades of colour. One hill had a fort atop, and Maria asked me what the story was. I couldn't remember exactly, but I told her how there were some Iron Age, Bronze Age and Roman forts along the estuary. She looked at me in awe, 'You mean there are structures that old and you haven't bothered to remember their stories?' Maria knew all the stories of Lisbon, they were woven into her Fado repertoire, and she treasured their sharing.

I felt relief when we met river-height again, safer beside my old friend than judging from above. The view felt kinder this way, less like I was conquering and more as if I was an intimate part of the estuary's course. We crossed the River Amble, and amble it did – a river after my own heart. I felt a tenderness toward it, tucked safely by marshy banks and nestled by miniature stone walls.

'They used to boat seaweed, sand and coal along here, then bring grain back down,' I told Maria, as amazed as her that I remembered such information.

'But it's so small,' Maria said, and I told her how they'd only boated at spring tides. Maria was fascinated in the practicalities of a river – how it could move useful things from the sea into land, and vice versa. I'd never really thought about it; the landscape had been part of the furniture.

As we neared Wadebridge, Maria kept repeating how green the ride had been. It shouldn't have surprised me – her land was parched and yellow – but I too was shocked at the vividness of it all.

We checked into our B&B, cooing over the fluffy, white towels, then headed to explore Wadebridge centre. Instead of tourist stops, we found interior design and kitchenware shops – leaving us fantasising how we'd decorate our first house, as though décor would solve the problem of in which country or even town this would be. We followed the sounds of singing to a locals' pub where a group of men were sharing shanties. I concentrated on my fish and chips while Maria made buddies and in no time was joining in the chorus. 'These songs tell the histories of your sea,' she cried, flushed face as she settled to eat chips gone cold.

The next morning, we joined the Camel Trail to start our return to Padstow. I felt far from home, though only ten kilometres, which made Lisbon feel epochs away. The sound of traffic on the bridge over the Camel just outside Wadebridge was serene, white noise fading into the background as we rode away from it – a rushing, rumbling, whirring – industry left behind.

Maria was wearing a pair of denim shorts and a

vest top, braving the April sun which shone bright but barely cut the surface. I was sure it should be the other way around – Brits stripped down to sandals and skirts at the first sight of spring – but Maria was embracing everything. The river beside us had narrowed from the wide-open mouth we'd seen the day before. Here, it was a tube heading into the stomach of the land. Deep mud banks rose either side of this sliver of water, giving way to marshy bits of land. There were swans, ducks, gulls walking the edges. 'What are those ones called?' asked Maria, pointing at some small, white birds with long skinny legs as we cycled past, but to her disappointment I couldn't remember their names. I was losing my native tongue.

The sky felt huge, blue, open, everything appearing wider around the riverway. Maria liked the snake lines across the mud where water channelled in, beside which were paths of footprints where morning dogwalkers had trailed. The mud was smooth like fresh, wet clay spread on a potter's board. Birds were drinking and wading – Wadebridge – the name had always seemed bland but now had a new flavour.

There were regularly placed benches and cut-throughs to beaches and Maria took each as an invitation to stop. I swallowed my impatience and followed her down the paths. The beaches were lined by succulents and sea spinach, with slate, cliffy sides and small oak trees overhanging. The landscape seemed spread out rather than up – low lying and immense – and I was grateful for Maria making me stop and see. She took me in her arms for a hug. 'Isn't it beautiful?' she asked, and I nodded.

The edge of the bike trail was banked by a tall wall, thickly quilted with ivy and couch grass. I noted the fern, primrose, nettles, three-cornered leek, and found a deep sense of satisfaction as each name was recalled; a language re-discovered. It brought the same thrill as learning Portuguese had, this feeling that a world was opening up to me.

As the path went on, the tall banks fell away, and we could see little alleys of water break off on each side. I took a liking to these, how they took their own route, and wished I could follow them. 'That's just like you,' said Maria when I told her, 'you want to be everywhere, but look where we are now!'

We stopped on one bench to eat an apple and stared at Bodmin Moor in the distance, hills turning blue, grey, dark and mountainous. 'We should cycle there,' I said to Maria, and she rested her head on my shoulder saying, 'Next time meu amor, next time.'

We cycled so slow we may as well have been walking, but this was Maria's nature – moving as though in burning sun. At yet another bench, Maria threw her bike down and summoned me to the water's edge. There we found a shipwrecked boat, faded blue outer and ragged green fishing net hung at its side. Maria conjured stories of how it might have ended up there – a pirate ship, a dead fishing fleet, a flood. I told her this river had been used for carrying goods for centuries, though not today.

'Coal, slate, sand—' I began to list.

'Don't be so boring,' said Maria, 'This boat was full of jewels.'

As we returned to our bikes, Maria pointed at the hills on the other side, 'Look, like giant breasts,' she laughed, and they were – formed to perfection with Friesian cows grazing. We were just about to push off again when another perfect formation passed on our other side. A couple, running, dressed in Lycra, perfect bodies defined by the tight fabric, smiles happy and smug. 'Let's follow them,' Maria said, 'maybe their contentment will rub off on you.'

We cycled slowly behind until they stopped at a little shack selling coffee. Maria directed us to the bench next to theirs and ordered what they ordered – two iced lattes – despite normally avoiding caffeine. I pointed out to her dandelion, buttercup, alexanders, red campion, but she was more interested in eavesdropping.

After learning the couple's names (Andy and Rosie), and hearing them argue about what to make for dinner, Maria was satisfied our lives lived up to theirs and announced we could move on. I pointed out the plantain, wild strawberries, bluebells, stitchwort – on a roll and unable to stop as the words came back to me. Maria was unimpressed and pointed out the mountains of slate instead, 'What is this about?' she asked.

I tried to explain something I'd remembered from primary school, 'Cornwall was a mining county, and, in this area, they mined slate. This trail was a railway line and, I think, it transported the slate down to Wadebridge.'

'And they just left it like this?' Maria exclaimed, gesturing at the piles of black, flattened stones.

We stopped to look at another beach. Maria was crashing after the caffeine, so we lay down on a sand of slate – grey, shingle, crushed together with shells. The sound of water was lapping as the tide filled the riverbed up. Maria dozed, nose tucked into my armpit, as I propped my head up with my other hand and watched a heron wait patiently to fish, feathers blending into the paling view.

When Maria woke, I was eager to show her what I had noticed: the seaweeds, little crabs, wild violet, and gorse. She kissed my cheek and said, 'Yes, this is your home, I hear you.'

We cycled on, blue-grey water on our right and craggy rock edges with green-brushed tops. What looked like some abandoned mining towers were on our left, as familiar to me as the sea. The river had opened into a huge, wide waterway and I could imagine the Roman boats travelling down, delivering goods. Humans had always looked beyond their doorsteps, but had they thought about the effects of doing so?

We stopped for a late lunch on a long slate beach, and I wondered aloud at how my homeland was built from its own ingredients – lime, slate, granite, sand. Maria pulled out two bottles of Doom Bar and said, 'Cheers to your homeland,' opening them both and then passing me one.

'When did you buy these?' I asked.

'While you were choosing paint colours in Wadebridge. I wanted to taste your local drink and compare it to my country's port.'

Drowsy from ale and filled with sandwiches and a deep, warming happiness, we gathered ourselves for the last stretch to Padstow. We biked over a large, industrial bridge, peering tipsily through its diagonals and triangles of metal. I felt myself sloshed around as below us the water entered the cheeks of the river before the mouth that would spit it out. 'Let us be free, like the water!' Maria called into the salty air.

As we rounded the corner, Padstow sprung up in the distance – nothing like Lisbon. Rising on a hill, yes, but white-fronted and modern-looking. Still, my tummy turned, and I realised I was excited to be back.

Clouds passed shadows across the hills on the opposite bank while fields flanked the side of the path. The town closed in. 'Will I be catching the plane back alone?' asked Maria, her eyes no longer laughing.

'I had been thinking the same earlier in the week.' I smiled. I reached out a hand to touch hers, 'Question is, will we be able to stay in either?'

'For now,' Maria said, closing her eyes, 'and that is all we have.'

There we found a shipwrecked boat, faded blue outer and ragged green fishing net hung at its side. Maria conjured stories of how it might have ended up there – a pirate ship, a dead fishing fleet, a flood.

AUTHOR

Polly Roberts

To gain inspiration for my short story, Trading Places, I packed my car with camping gear and the dog and set off to walk the Camel Trail. What struck me was the balance in this Area of Oustanding Natural Beauty of natural and human history - the old mining infrastructure, the marks of a busy trading route, the hilltop forts, and of course the flow of tourists and dog walkers, all nestled on the banks of the magnificent estuary itself. I felt instantly this was a human story, but as with any human story it must be defined by its scenery. The plants along the Camel estuary are numerous, the landscape and the weather varied, I found my eyes called to wonders both tiny and large - mussels then rolling hills, butterflies then white sandy beach. There is so much to admire and explore here, and a rich history to read into, I was honoured to pay a small homage with my story.

THE RETURNERS

by Annamarie Murphy
(Section 04 - Carnewas to Stepper Point)

Henry Trevear has returned to Carnewas. Things have changed, he thinks, things he must impart in a letter to his dear wife Lily.

The taste on the air is salt and sky.

The birds are spoilt for choice of where to land, as there is so much cliff, so many headlands, so much sky. But no trees for them to nest in to speak of. It's a naked kind of beauty here.

Walking down the path to Whitestone Cove, marram grass brushes his legs, and the dog-rose barks pink.

Time has clawed the cliffs, storms have licked the earth, the land is bitten by winds. And there are the islands. Pendarves, Redcove, Queen Bess Rock. They long for the land to which they once belonged, but the spaces in between them are further apart than he remembers.

Surely Pendarves Island was joined to the cliff last time he was here?

Surely Queen Bess Rock looked more like Queen Bess? Where is her nose?

He must ask Lily if she remembers.

These rocks, grandly called islands, are layer cakes of geology, stripes of history, and he wouldn't be surprised if there are creatures in the rock, some fishes ready to grow legs and walk the earth.

Such thoughts are blasphemous, though who can see his thoughts out here?

He has come to inspect the lighthouse and day-marks along this stretch of coast, and the roads and footpaths that lead to them. It's a long walk to Stepper Point and much to inspect on the journey – but it's good to be back.

He must send his reports to Sir James Douglass, engineer and master builder of lighthouses on impossible rocks.

It's midday, and he must set a pace if he's to get to Trevose before dark, for he has maps to draw and entries to write, and he is hoping that the keepers there will have gotten word of his visit and have at least supper of some kind to greet him.

Nobody about. Except behind him, coming up from Trerathick Point, is a snaking line of something.

Men. Possibly from the direction of the old shaft.

Nobody knows when those workings were last mined. Not in his day certainly. But maybe they'd found a new lode of iron and copper and re-opened it? God knows, and he truly did, for there is much need for employment round these parts.

So close to the edge, those workings. Too near to the howl of the ocean. He preferred to look out across the briny, not to tunnel under it like mole-men.

As they come closer, he can see they look weary, but he can hear a faint tune on the wind.

'Where shall my wondering soul begin,

How shall I all to heaven aspire?'

An appropriate song for this place, and their voices are fine. But now they are gone. Maybe back to the hamlet of cottages in Carnewas? Down some path he didn't know? Or resting with their croust behind one of the ancient stone walls?

The two eyeholes in the granite skull beyond Bedruthan always make him shiver. Their sockets are sightless, but their stare is cold, and there is some myth around them that he can't remember, but Lily would know, as she told the children the story. They always claimed they like to be frightened, but then they could not sleep, and would creep into his and Lily's bed saying that the eyes had winked at the them and that the cliff had a mouth and had said it would swallow them whole. And and and …

Grown now. Lucky to be grown. Lucky to have seen them grown.

'How great thou art …' How did that tune go again? Nobody to ask but the circling sparrow hawk, and it is concentrating on a rabbit, and there is no bush, no furze for the poor creature to hide, and soon that rabbit will get a bird's eye view of the St Eval moors and this ragged coast.

By mid-afternoon he has reached Booby's Bay.

On the way to the beach he sees samphire and sea-spinach. A delicacy some say – but if picked wrong, tough as old boots. Mind, in desperate times, good in a stew.

There are flags whipping by a wooden hut, as if trying to escape their poles. He can't remember the flags, and they are bright in colour. Yellow and red.

There is someone out at sea. They are paddling on something, trying to ride the wild waves. In his day, it was coffin lids or a plank, and only the lads would do it, but this looks to be a woman. She shouldn't be out there. Not in this weather.

'Hello. Are you in trouble?'

Thy power throughout the universe displayed.

'Hold on. I'll take off my boots.'

But she has ridden the wave, and skids onto the blonde sand, and picks up her board shaped like a fish and walks towards the wooden hut shaking the sea from her hair. Henry Trevear is not sure what he's seen, but the sun is beating down and his thirst fierce, so he drinks from his bottle and rests against a slatey rock.

When he wakes it is late afternoon, and still a few miles

to go before he reaches Trevose head.

The wind is up.

The sun setting.

It is after dusk when he reaches the lighthouse. The moon is out and catches the tower, making it seem like some eastern minaret. It seems to have been repainted.

Sir Douglass will be pleased to hear that.

In his last report Sir Douglass had stated of Trevose: 'The machinery is keeping perfect time. Everything connected with the changes is quite satisfactory. As the night is foggy, I have given instructions to light six wicks.'

'Hello. Henry Trevear here.'

Silence.

Not asleep surely? Or worse, drunk? Drunkenness is sometimes the occupational hazard of keepers.

He climbs the winding staircase to the lamps. There is no smell of oil and wick. No smeech from the flame, just the clear corneas of the lamps rotating. He cannot see how they are turning, who or what is turning them.

And where are the men?

Everything is as it was. The curved furniture. The sleeping quarters. The stove. The hob.

But no sign of the keepers. No boots. No oilskins. No smells.

That was it. No smells of cooking. Of boots. Of wick.

Henry climbs the stairs and lies on a bunk and wishes he was home with Lily.

Isaiah Pender, Bosun, *Britannia.* Wrecked off Padstow,

1805. Some of us saved.

Benny Twopence, ship's boy, *The Fanny*. Harlyn Bay, 1810. We was all lost.

Erwin Vandrop, Captain, *The Voorspoed*. 1901, rescued from here: breeches buoy.

Eliza and Mary Pitee, daughters of Hezekiah Pitee, head keeper of St Augustine Lighthouse. 1873, drowned playing near the shore, though Mother had told us not to.

Symons, Murphy, Carey and Du Barra. We disappeared from Flannan, and still no one knows why. We do though, eh lads?

Whole crew, the John Taylor, all lost off Park Head. Some of us might have been saved if this place had been built earlier. Still, better late than never.

Let's drink to that! Who's this now?

Henry Trevear. I'm Henry Trevear. Inspector of lighthouses and day-marks for Trinity House.

Trinity House! A toast to them! Won't you join us, Henry Trevear?

No. No thank you. Sir Douglass is waiting for my report. I'm on my way to Stepper Point day-mark.

Sir Douglass. He deserves a toast. Where would we be without Sir Douglass?

Henry Trevear takes his leave in a hurry, for he must make his sketches of the state of the day-mark, and he has a room booked in Annie Nance's boarding house in Padstow.

This time, he must be careful not to go near Round

Hole at Trevone. It's an extraordinary phenomenon, he wrote to Lily, a sunken sea cave, most perfectly round, the roar from within it like a thousand cannons, and when you look into it, the sensation of falling is overwhelming.

He hears a last toast, then the rising of a song as he leaves.

Here's to us lads, and ladies. The Returners.

'Where shall my wondering soul begin?

How shall I all to heaven aspire?'

It is after dusk when he reaches the lighthouse. The moon is out and catches the tower, making it seem like some eastern minaret. It seems to have been repainted.

AUTHOR

Annamaria Murphy

On my walk from Carnewas to Stepper Point it was the geology of the rocks and cliffs that struck me. You could see the layers of time in the coloured strata, and likewise the paths close to the edge, where miners must have walked, and now ramblers, surfers, bird watchers, all pitch themselves against the winds and crumbling pathways. Also, the sheer endeavour of building lighthouses, now mostly unmanned, lent themselves to a kind of ghost story. I always feel in Cornwall when I walk with my notebook, that history, memory and the present walk with me, and that time plays its tricks.

Author photograph: Steve Tanner

PERRAN IN THE SANDS

by Emma Timpany

(Section - 05 St Agnes)

The sand, the sea, the stream, the spring. By the well, thin rags hang limp from branches of thorn, and lark song falls like water poured. Humped dunes stretch to the beach, leading the way into the wideness of waves, the horizon's white line.

I crouch by black rocks loosening limpets, chipping away with a battered bronze knife to part them from their home scars, dropping them like stones into my flax basket. The worst job of all, fit for the youngest, fit for a girl, my brothers tell me. But sometimes good comes out of bad, like molten tin from blackest ore, because if I hadn't been limpet picking, I wouldn't have seen the man.

He floats on the sea, carried on a boat made of tight-stretched hide so small that he seems to rest on the waves themselves. Where the stream threads the beach with sweet water, he hauls himself out of the surf, dragging the round vessel behind him by a rope. Once clear of the swash, he lies his great body down on the sand, while the sun, hot and low, steams his damp clothes dry. Then he half-walks and half-crawls, drops to his knees and drinks from the stream on all fours like a sheep.

The musk scent of hawthorn cuts the heat, though the wind here shaves the bushes so they hide their flowers inside a net of leaves. In the sky, beneath fine strands of horsetail clouds, a raven draws black circles in the high-blown blue; its croaking seems to rouse him. Now he sits with his back to the dunes and faces the waves, shaking his head as if astonished that the sea has delivered him here, and then he lies on his back and laughs at the sky.

I wonder what Father will make of him, what my brothers will say. He isn't like our usual visitors from across the western water, bringing copper to trade for our tin, or those from further north with their furs, or those from the south, from Armorica. He has no idea I'm here. I'm used to going unseen, belly low to the dunes, blending with soft steps into the grasses in my lichen-grey clothes. The sand keeps secrets, trapping sound, but footsteps leave a trail of holes that anyone can follow. I creep as close as I dare until I am looking down on him, at his great ribs rising and falling, the sound of his snoring a rumble like sea rocks banging in the hollow of his chest.

Before long I hear them calling, whistling for me as they whistle for the goats. In my hurry, I rinse the limpets carelessly and, back at the enclosure, Mother divides them out. When my father bites down on grit, I receive a clout, so I say nothing about the man.

He's been here for a while now, has made a camp on the verdant green, on turf close cropped by the soft mouths of our sheep and goats. Sometimes he shows us his oval stone carved with the image of a tree, one thick straight trunk cut by one thick branch. He fills his cup with water from the spring and sings in his great voice before the sun has risen and the cold morning air sweeps us with its damp, sandy brush. Night animals creep closer to the fire he's lit – badger, boar and fox – and I creep closer, too, to hear the strange words he speaks, his salt and granite song.

In the evening, Father and the other men talk to him. In the late light, I see him lead them to the top of the dunes. I see him spread his hands wide and then pat them down – soft, soft, soft – as if he were somehow able to smooth flat the blue blanket of the sea. Beside them he seems so big, more forest tree than man. He says this place is special, blessed, that a new god has sent him here to us, that we are special, too. He talks about an everlasting life, of a home in the sky to live in after death. Soon they say he is allowed to stay here with us, not be just another trader passing through. I see him collect stones and materials to build a cell, as small and round as his coracle.

While my father and brothers are fishing, I tend the

animals. I'm out on the dunes when he whistles my tune to the goats and they run to him, so I run, too. The goats jostle each other to push their warm flanks against his big thighs, begging for a scratch around their horns. He talks and sings to them as he does to us, and down they settle in the sparse grass to doze in the shade of his cell.

He places his big hand on my head, chanting words I don't understand, and then he raises his arms above his head like a cup, rocks back and forth and sings. He is always singing; sometimes he drops his head and stands or kneels singing in the stream and the spring, and sometimes in the waves.

Word spreads as far as his wide-open arms, as if those distant are called here by his song. They have heard that he performs wonders, that he made a stork sing, made cold water warm, caused snow to fall from a hot blue sky. That he restored sight to the blind and life to the dead. That his mother, Wingella, conceived him by dreaming that she saw a star clearer than all others fall into her mouth.

I have not seen him perform wonders. I only see what I have always seen: the beauty of the pale sand pillows, the soft grey of the marram, the birds – meadow pipit, linnet, skylark – dipping in the green, two silver-blue butterflies touching feet and tumbling above the turf, to break apart a breath above the earth.

So many come to hear him speak and sing in his funny tongue, he starts building a chapel of wattle and daub, as oval as our enclosure but with a roof of thatch, made fast with those great hands. Around the oval stone he carried through the waves, he builds an altar, flat and strong, on which he rests a cloth, a cup, a copper bell, a cross of bone.

Before Beltane, he beckons us with song, saying his god's son is risen from the dead. He strikes a spark to light the fire he calls the lumen Christ, and lifts his cup and drinks sweet water from it, while sparks fly up, flashing orange before melting into night. Heat pours from the wood, as the fire builds itself into a flaming tower. I add my limpets to the feast, scoop out gold flesh, then toss the empty grey-white shell on the midden heap of blue-black mussels, fish skeletons and bones gnawed clean of meat.

As in life, so in death. Like all the living creatures he encounters, in eternity we wish to lie as near him as the fine gold sand the north wind lifts here from the beach. To hold us in this shifting earth, they rest stones, flat and heavy, on our feet and heads and chests, with lighter stones placed beneath. They cross our leg bones and lie us with our heads east and our feet west, on the sun path from dawn to dusk. Some of us lie curled on our right sides in cists with walls and roofs of slate, open to the earth beneath.

When he dies, they bury his great body under the oratory altar but keep his head apart in a reliquary to parade through the settlements on holy days and feasts. With it, they carry his bronze-hooked staff, his copper bell, his tin cup, his cross of bone. Over time, his oratory is rebuilt of slate and moorland quartz, mortared by sand and fine white clay. For fifteen hundred years, pilgrims come here, to him and us, to rest and pray, because he was the first to tell the people of this island about the truth, the light, the way.

Each year, the sea rises and the land diminishes. Each day the waves wage their long war and the land resists, but, in the end, the moon-driven waves always win. As the sea craves the shore, so the dunes crave the land, their sands as unstoppable as the tide. Year by year, week by week, grain by grain, they wrap the oratory walls in their pale embrace.

After a thousand years, the oratory is lost to the sand, but even the mightiest dune cannot cross water. The people build a new church across the stream, inside our ancient burial ground where the oldest of us lie with weapons, ornaments and food, ready for the afterlife in a world underground or on islands in the western sea. Our menhir is re-carved into a cross, though it still looks like a stone man.

When mining takes the stream water, the dunes advance and take the new church into their unyielding softness. The people take down the walls and tower and carry the stones inland. We tens of thousands are left here below the sand, beneath the wind.

When the oratory's west wall breaks through a dune hollow, we are dug out with it to lie open to the sky, bathed once more in light, a vast bone harvest, our white teeth flowers in the dusk. The oratory is looted, its altar stone stolen, everything stripped bare. People take our bones to keep as souvenirs, keep bits of us in cupboards and in jars. Those who return us are left in peace, the others never forgiven.

They rebury us eventually, build a fence to keep the looters out and then a concrete shell, curve-roofed as a cave, is raised over the oratory's stones. Inside, rainwater collects and the ground water rises, but the people wade through it to lay flowers and light candles in the darkness. Now the oratory lies open to the sky again, green locks of water crow's-foot dotted with star-white flowers swirling in black water, and the sweet, ashy scent of wild mint lingers in damp corners.

We don't mind the water. It touches some of us beneath the sand. It rises and falls around us, reminding us of what it felt like to have lungs, to stand in the air and breathe the salt wind, to gasp as we pulled a catch from the boats, to holler at the naughtiest of goats, to laugh and lift our voices up in song, bright and high as larks, the sound of life itself pouring from our mouths.

Now, each day, the living pass, no longer whistling to their stock but to their dogs and kids. Ponies with walnut-coloured coats graze the army land beyond the wire. Rabbits hop and linnets dip. On the sea wind, a raven shoots the sky, its blackness turning white as it dissolves into the sun.

Seasons cycle by with the opening and falling of the

leaves; east and west along the coast, the pattern of headland and beach repeats, repeats, repeats. Fires are lit in high places, on the pointed hill they call St Agnes Beacon, and we remember the two purifying need-fires we drove the sheep and goats between at Beltane, how we all ran between the fires, too, for healing or for better luck.

Few but the dogwalkers come in the winter storms, when the cold burns and the flying sand grains scratch cheeks and hands raw, where the rain hurls flat and fast, and the sea wind rules like an iron king. We sing to them sometimes, our voices blurring in the howl and whisper of the gale. Sometimes they stop and shiver, pull their scarves around their necks and zip their jackets tighter, then call their dogs and run back to the road, their cars, the light and warmth of home.

In early spring, the people come to stand and sing, carrying his flag and, for us, armfuls of sun-bright daffodils. We ask them to talk to us, and while they talk, we listen. We have always listened. We take their prayers to keep, to echo amongst us like precious shells whispering with sea-sound. We keep the secrets of their souls, their hopes, their fears, their anger, and their pain. We lie in their blood like mead and stir them fire warm. When they leave, we nestle in their clothing – a sprig of mint, a swirled snail shell, a tiny speck of grit. We understand that faith moves like the sand, that it both comes and goes.

The track leads down to the dunes. By a small stream hedged by hawthorn and elder, the budding spires of musk-pink agrimony. The sky's unbroken blue is a portent of late-morning heat. The tall pole on the dune is stark, its true shape hidden until the bar comes into view. A cross. A magpie stops to rest on it, its piebald feathers wet with sun. Nearby, snug in the towans, the stone bones of two ruins lie open to the sky.

Today, a border collie noses through the oratory's open gate and splashes the dark water, leaving paw prints in the entrance's damp sand, dipping its head to drink. A small plane cuts the sky, and the surfer girls come running past again, wetsuits pulled down to hips, bikini tops against bare skin, one dark-haired and one blond, with plaited hair tailing down her back. They hold two surfboards designed with blue-black swirling galaxies of distant stars. We sing to them to come and see us and this time they stop as if they've felt us, or maybe seen the woman perched above us on the sand lip.

'How can we have passed this every day,' the fair one with the Irish accent asks, 'and not noticed the building before?'

'I'm so unobservant,' the dark-haired one says. 'I could walk the same way for years and never notice a thing.'

They read the information board aloud while bugs crawl up the seated woman's back.

'In the 5th century ad, St Piran founded the first Christian church on mainland Britain here.'

'An ancient site, surrounded by a vast graveyard.'

'One skeleton of giant size was found.'

'And a woman with a child in her arms was buried beneath the doorstep.'

'Aw.'

They read on in silence, then look at the remains of the oratory, old and new. On the tallest remnant of concrete, purple graffiti swirlingly spells 'SMILE'. They gaze at the hair-like waterweed, at the prickly sow-thistle topping the wall, then off they jog, carrying painted constellations down paths of sand.

Early this morning, a thrush used the pediment in the old church to bash a snail's shell from its flesh. The shell lies empty now, and porcelain pale. Foxgloves stand; wild roses grow creamy and low amongst bird's-foot trefoil. Over the surface of the oldest cross on this island, a mask of lichen grows, glaucous grey on the east side and bright mustard on the west. At its base a stand of iris, and the dark green tendrils and deep purple flowers of deadly nightshade spill onto the turf. Light catches in the grass stems, tall and slender. The great heartbeat of the tide that never ceases is crisp and clear as the new moon in a violet sky.

Yesterday someone dropped a red rose in the dark mirror of the oratory's water. There it floats, a flower for a lover. So many love him still and I ask them to love us all as well, his faithful, the sea of bones surrounding him, the proof of our devotion.

Remember us when you come here, as numerous as the plants which sparkle in the green; see us in the grass flowers, hear us in the whisper of the surf. A myriad of souls, lucky to rest in this eternal place. Beyond us a silver pathway lies on the evening sea, the light of goodness shining in the black, a cross of molten tin which pours from burning stone. Feel us, cool and heavy, in the grains which fill your palm, our faith as bright and endless as the sand.

In the late light, I see him lead them to the top of the dunes. I see him spread his hands wide and then pat them down – soft, soft, soft – as if he were somehow able to smooth flat the blue blanket of the sea.

AUTHOR

Emma Timpany

I visited St Piran's Oratory on a bright May morning when the air was full of skylark song and tiny flowers sprinkled the sandy grass.

Set within a prehistoric enclosure and nestled in a 5,000-year-old sand dune system, the remains of the building lie open to the sky and its interior, filled with dark ground water, is mirror-like.

The oldest Christian site on mainland Britain is quiet, otherworldly, and deeply peaceful, a rare 'thin place' where the barrier between heaven and earth dissolves. Wildly beautiful and inspiring, the home of Cornwall's patron saint provides solace for the soul and heart.

by Clare Howdle

(Section 06 - Godrevy to Portreath)

The girl is to arrive on a Saturday under a bruised sky. Rain begins to spit on Violet's drive to the station. By the time she reaches the barrier it's hard and constant, drawing out the scent of grass and earth to mingle with the brackish breeze. It had been blue skies that morning. Blue skies and bird song, and she had thought, how fitting, and she had thought, this will help, I'm sure. Not now though. Now the bank of cloud that threatened as dawn broke has won its fight with the sun and taken hold. Such a shame.

When the girl gets off the train, Violet keeps her distance. Watches her chest swell with a deep breath, her frown loosen as she blinks long and slow. Raindrops spread across the girl's face. She wipes them clear. Her eyes flicker, sun to shadow.

There's no one else waiting, so when the girl sees a woman sheltering at the far edge of the platform she steps forward, breaks a tentative smile. Violet holds her umbrella out and the girl ducks under it, but it's too small for two strangers and they are squashed together, closer than either of them would like, penned in by the rain.

Violet speaks first, an attempt to ease the awkwardness. She apologises for the weather because it feels like the only thing she has. She takes the girl's rucksack, and they rush to the car.

On the journey back to the house, Violet wants to talk to the girl some more. She knows they can talk, have already, on scheduled calls she'd prepared for with a list of questions. What's your favourite colour, what do you do in your spare time, do you have enough food, are you coping just now? And the girl smiled and answered and said she was okay, a little scared but so happy that Violet was making it possible for her to leave, giving her somewhere safe to stay. This is not like that. She has no plan. No facilitator. The girl's family is not in the background smiling and saying thank you for doing this, for being there. It does not feel as simple now. She does not know what to say.

Violet searches hard, harder. Comes up with only small talk.

How was the trip?

The trip was fine.

Were you looked after?

I was.

Have you spoken to your parents?

Not yet.

On the coast, the rain abates. A line of light cracks the sky, its brightness lifting the leaden sea to jade. It is going to be a beautiful evening, Violet offers, slowing down to take the bends of the tarmac road as it peters out into dusty track.

The girl smiles, but it is tight and hollow.

Violet's mother's house is small. Set between cauliflower fields and towan slopes capped with grass, brambles. Sand piles on its doorstep, salt burrows into its slats, crystalises in circles on its glass.

You're in here, Violet says, opening the door to her mother's room. She has cleared out the medical equipment, bought new green bedsheets, painted one of the walls green, too, to make the girl feel at home.

It's not much, but I hope you like it. I chose your favourite colour.

The girl presses her lips together, dips her head in gratitude.

Silence trembles like taut fishing wire. When it gets too much, Violet asks if the girl is hungry, says she'll make some dinner. In the kitchen she leans heavily on the countertop, tries to pull herself together. She stares across the shifting sand. The wind is up a little and the marram grass flails in it, throwing light and shade across the kitchen wall. The rain will have brought the snails out, Violet thinks, finally rousing herself to get on, chopping an onion, boiling water. And now the sun has returned with the wind, it's drying the grass, the air.

A good night for it.

A promising night.

While the meal is cooking, she checks her timetable. Still stuck to the fridge, with magnets brought back from summer holidays she took her mother on. Dartmouth, Lyme Regis, Westwood Ho! Never too far because they had to get back, her mother always said. Miss one night, maybe two, but no more.

Right to the end, they would do it. Violet's arm under her mother's shoulder, helping her down into the towans' wells, the damp give of the sand beneath their feet, the final throes of a reed warbler's song spinning through the air. And they would stand and listen to the birds, the wind, the sea, waiting for the fullness of the night to drop. For the moment it would happen.

Miss one night. Maybe two. No more.

Violet has missed so many now, she's lost track.

She runs her finger across the timetable. Sunset, 9:20 p.m. tonight. Waxing crescent moon. Calming weather. Peak conditions.

Her throat tightens. She picks up a pencil and draws a firm line through the date, like all the dates above it. She can't bring herself to count them up. Can't bear to think what her mother would say.

She lays the table, calls out, waits. Keeps waiting.

No movement.

No sound.

Outside the bedroom door she stays quiet. She doesn't understand the words, but the cadence of the girl's voice is familiar, true. The pace, the pauses, the pitch.

Sadness.

Solitude.

She clenches her fingers into a fist, raises it to knock but can't seem to do it. The tray of food teeters on her hip. What can she say that will help? She doesn't have anything useful to give.

She places the tray on the floor and backs away.

It's dark by the time she hears the click of the handle, the creak of the floorboards outside the girl's room as the tray is taken. In the silence of the lounge she listens, eyes down, trying to ignore her mother's chair, still turned toward the sea as if at any moment she might come in, sit, start lacing up her boots, telling Violet to get a wriggle on, that the night won't wait. The bedroom door closes. She imagines the girl upstairs, alone. Eating cold pasta. Staring through the window into the darkness, where the stars are not hers and the sand susurrates in endless waves.

This is not how she hoped it would be.

This is not it at all.

Another hour passes. The moon blinks. The towans call. But she cannot free her feet from the floor. Cannot work out how to move forward. She pulls the dogeared notebook from the drawer and studies the last entry, made a year ago.

24 June. Gwithian Towans, 50.21795 N, 5.39773 W, 1-f.

She runs her finger across the paper to feel the imprint of her mother's scrawl. The truth of it sticks in her throat, a hard-worn rock smoothed down to a shine from the months and days and hours of trying to swallow it away.

The next morning, the girl is up early. Already in the kitchen when Violet comes down, she has made tea. Her face still carries pillow marks, her eyes are puffy and raw.

Did you sleep? Violet says, reaching for the milk from the girl and pouring a dash into her cup. Were you comfortable?

I could hear the sea. It is loud here.

You'll get used to it. I've lived here all my life. I can't sleep without it now.

The girl takes in the countertop pulling away from the wall, the broken tiles, the cupboard held up by a wooden strut, the rusting taps.

Where is your family?

Violet sees her looking. The colour rises in her cheeks.

It was only ever me and my mother. And she was the one that looked after the house … until she couldn't.

Violet knows she should give the girl more, can see she is waiting for it. That she should tell her she is alone now, invited her here exactly for that reason. Because she heard it was a way to do her bit, to make a difference. Because she had the room. But also, if she's honest, because she knows people are willing her to do something, anything, to move on. It's time to move on, they've all been saying. So this is her trying. Company. That's what people do, isn't it, when moving on is required? Seek company. Find solace. Begin again. Except it doesn't feel right or real and all of it is so, so heavy. How can she talk of any of this with the girl? Of love and loss? Of the strain and pressure, the release, the guilt? The effort and exhaustion of pretending to be fine because it's what's expected? It's too much for anyone to have to hear.

The girl's brow furrows. She finds Violet's eye, holds it. Would you like to walk?

The look on her face is deep and purposeful, her lips parted as if she is also trying to catch the words she wants to say, but they're refusing to let her.

She drains her cup. Come on, she says. Let's walk. It is a new day.

Outside the sun is already high and hazy. Seagulls wheel and screech. The girl shades her eyes and looks out to sea. Breathes.

Violet leads them to the cliff edge where tourists and daytrippers park, unload, carry their brightly coloured windbreaks and cool bags past the lifeguard hut and through the rocks, to the beach.

The track here used to go straight down, Violet says, pointing at all the cars lined up along the top. When my mother was little, they would drive right onto the sand.

She hadn't meant to say it, wishes she could take it back, but the girl's expression has already lifted with the hint of a smile. She leans in.

It has changed a lot?

Violet watches the lines of swell advance, dark shadows rising, peaking, then toppling into white water and rumbling to the shore.

In some ways, she says hurriedly, moving them along. In others, not at all.

They stop for a rest by the ruins of a sand processing plant. Derelict for many years, but still standing proud, its concrete warms their backs as they sit. The silence condenses. Awkward. Layered. The girl bites her lip, digs her hands through the sand.

What is this?

She pincers something between her fingers, holds it up to the light. It's tiny, pale, almost transparent. It glistens.

And in Violet's throat, the hard-worn rock rises, and sticks, and traps her words inside. But this time she thinks of the girl and why she is here and what it means to her. What Violet has promised, should be trying to do. She nips the skin on her arms until it stings. Uses it to feel her way back to herself. She must do better.

It's a snail shell. You'll see hundreds of them if you look closely.

The girl begins to dig again, finds more, lining them up on the grass and counting as she goes.

Why are there so many?

They've been eaten.

By birds?

Maybe. Also by glow worms. By their larvae.

What are glow worms?

The question hangs in the air, just out of reach. Violet stretches for it, but the hard, worn rock presses against her windpipe, steals her breath. She sees the brightness start to fade from the girl's face, so reaches a little higher, a little further, until her fingertips find purchase on the question. She pulls it to her, bites on it, swallows it down. And its pressure pushes the hard, worn rock aside and its power creates a little gap. The smallest of spaces. Just enough. To breathe again. To talk.

They actually aren't worms at all. They're beetles, which can make little lights with their bodies. There's a colony of them right here on the towans, has been for decades. There's a chance – she splits a clump of marram grass, pulling the blades down to the root – look, there, see?

A small beetle, long and thin. And a larva. Two.

The girl squints. But they are not glowing?

It's the females that glow the strongest. At night and only for a few weeks.

They lose their light?

They don't live very long. Three years as larvae. Two weeks, at the most, fully grown. Because of their life cycle, they can lie unseen for years. But they don't go away. The snail shells are a sign they're still here.

How do you know so much about glow worms?

The girl picks up each shell as she speaks, cupping them in her palm before tipping them into her jeans pocket.

I used to go hunting for them.

To catch them?

To count them, keep a record. Some years we'd go a whole season only seeing one or two. Others we'd see twenty, thirty, forty a night.

Did you do it for a long time?

Since I was younger than you.

Why did you stop?

Violet releases the grass. She wants to tell the girl how every evening of every summer they would head into the towans, wait for the little lights to appear. How they would keep a log, type up the report at the end of the week and post it off somewhere. How it was only as an adult that she challenged it, a challenge that – when her mother died – fast petrified to stone. No one else cared about the glow worms. No one else even knew. So what was the point?

But the hard, worn rock pushes higher, higher, covering her tongue, filling her mouth. She cannot get rid of it so easily.

She dusts the sand off her clothes.

Enough rest. Let's get on.

They walk for another hour, more, down to the red river, over the headland by the lighthouse, up to Mutton Cove. The hedges brag of summer: cowslips, campions, montbretia, yellow, pink, shocking orange against the sky's infinite blue. Foxgloves tower and nettles shiver. Violet looks beyond the fields to the dark smudge on the skyline where Tehidy's ancient oaks claim the north cliffs, then back over the expanse of the bay to the towans where her mother's house battles against the sand. Such a varied landscape in such a small stretch. So much to explore, to know.

It is lucky to grow up here, the girl says, following Violet's gaze. You are so lucky.

That evening, when the girl goes to bed, Violet sits at the desk in the corner of the lounge. She runs her fingers over her mother's typewriter. There's still paper on the platen, still ribbon on the spool. So many reports, typed and sent. More permanent that way, her mother insisted. Out of our hands and into the world.

In her final days, when Violet's grief started to twist and turn before it had a right to, she asked her. On the towans, with the dark enveloping them. How do you know? That anyone is there? That anyone is bothered about what we see?

And her mother shook her head and smiled. She swayed to the melody of the sea.

I don't, she said. Not anymore. But we can't know everything. Why pay that any mind? The towans keep calling. And the little lights will glow. Some years more. Some years less. Who are we to ignore them?

That night in bed, her body drowning in a swathe of blankets, she asked Violet to open the window, so she could hear the sea.

My time's up, girl, she rasped, as she reached for Violet's hand, no light left in me. It's your time now.

Her words were barely distinguishable from the whisper of the waves.

Violet looks at the map above the desk, marks out the ruins where they stopped this afternoon, works out the coordinates. She presses the typewriter keys slowly. The gathered dust in the mechanism mutes each clack.

24 June. Gwithian Towans, South West Coast Path, 50.21865 n, 5.39534 w, 1-m, 2-l, by day.

Before bed, she cracks the girl's door ajar to check on her. Her body rises and falls with the embrace of sleep. On her bedside table the tiny, empty shells are lined up, one next to the other. They glint in the moonlight.

It's after midnight when Violet wakes. A hand on her arm, a gentle word in her ear.

Are you okay?

Her neck aches. Her spine cracks. She is back at the desk, her fingers on the typewriter keys.

The girl holds up a glass.

I came for water, I saw you here.

She looks over Violet's shoulder, screws up her eyes to try and make sense of the single line of letters and numbers Violet has typed.

Violet takes the paper from the roller and puts it aside.

We should go to bed, she sighs.

The girl sits on the chair in the window. Violet's mother's chair. She tilts her head as if listening to the sea. She parts her lips, pausing, catches the words she's been chasing.

I miss my family.

It's clear and whole and rings like glass.

Violet looks away, looks down, looks out into the night sky, anywhere to avoid the intensity of the girl's stare. She tries to say I'm sorry. She tries to say I understand, but it gets trapped like always, with no way of slipping free.

The girl runs her palms down her face. She reaches for the edge of the typed paper, looks at the sentence again.

Do you miss yours?

In the air between them, Violet hears the grass dance. The waves whisper. She closes her eyes and sees the sand ripple, the sun set, the crescent moon climb. She tastes the salt, feels the drop, lets it in. A little light flickers, glows. Just one. For them.

The hard, worn rock that's paralysed her for exactly one year slowly moves, a little back, a little lower, until there's more space than stone.

Violet nods, takes Nina's hand. For the first time since she invited this girl into her mother's home, her home, she understands what she's supposed to do.

The night is dark and empty, the towans claggy underfoot from another afternoon of rain. Violet leads Nina over the mounds and wells.

Where are we going?

Not much further.

What will we see?

Maybe nothing. I don't think that matters though. It's being here that counts.

Nina squeezes Violet's hand, Violet pulls her closer. They switch off their torches. The silence is not so threatening now, the distance that separates them not so far.

They focus on the grass, letting their eyes adjust to the fullness of the dark.

And they wait.

They stop for a rest by the ruins of a sand processing plant. SDerelict for many years, but still standing proud, its concrete warms their backs as they sit. The silence condenses. Awkward. Layered. The girl bites her lip, digs her hands through the sand.

AUTHOR

Clare Howdle

A sweep of glass stretching into sea mist. Towers of rain-pummelled sand taking a breath under an optimistic patch of blue. The silent prowess of the lighthouse brushed white against the rising dusk. The shelter of ancient trees clinging to ocean-worn cliffs. For as long as I can remember I've been drawn to Godrevy's coastal stretch, in all its seasons and shades. My family has lived in and loved this place for generations, and I feel its legacy. The creatures that make the towans their home, the people. It's in the smallest of interactions, a shell found in the sand, a dance of lights in the grass under moonlight, a rundown building, relic of industry, warming in the midday sun, that the most powerful of tales is told. Life in all its complexity is captured here, and invites you in. Come, dwell a while, it calls to us. Seek a fresh perspective.

by C. M. Davis
(Section 07 - West Penwith)

They came down from the farm in the late morning, along the coffin path to Saint Senara's. It was the only way. Below them the sea lay still; there hadn't been a wind for weeks. Above them, shadows on the ridge charted their slow progress towards the church. The path wound its way through gorse and rocky outcrops, but for the most part the slope was gentle.

Six carried the casket, and it was heavy, for in it lay both mother and child. Matthew, at fourteen, had begged in earnest to join in. The men had agreed, though they all knew he was too short, too much of a boy still, to do a proper job. But now he walked behind his big brother Luke, the smooth box of wood sitting solidly on their left shoulders. Their little company moved together yet apart, an insect creeping, Matthew thought, as they made their way down the hill.

It was another torrid day. The ground was parched, and as they pushed on, Luke's boots, well-shined by their mother, kicked up clouds of dust behind him that Matthew couldn't escape. To make matters worse, his best waistcoat was much too small. Made more than a year ago, now the fabric held him tight like a ladies' corset. This, and the sorrow balled up deeply behind his sternum, were beginning to make breathing arduous.

The six stayed in rhythm and the way began to level out. Matthew walked it every Sunday and knew that the church's tower would now be visible in the distance to the two at the front. To his right a calm sea, usually reassuring, but today too bright and too shiny to look at. If he looked down, though, the dust threatened to rise into his eyes. He settled on staring at the back of Luke's head, grateful not to be able to see his face. For the past three days he'd not looked like his brother anymore. The cheerful, proud young man now seemed brittle as cuttlefish bone, dimmed and almost disfigured by death. It wasn't right to lose a wife so young, Mother had said, as she'd come back into the kitchen with another untouched tray of bread and soup. He might never be the same again, and him only twenty. Who would've thought it, a lass so strong and well-made as Sarah-Jane?

Until then, the only person Matthew had known who'd

actually died was his grandmother. And it hadn't been at all the same. She'd gone in stages, shrinking steadily down into a tiny seed. She'd eaten soup for a month, then nothing for two weeks and died quietly one Tuesday afternoon two winters ago. Sarah-Jane was robust and cheerful up to the very day she'd gone. When her waters had broken on the kitchen floor at lunchtime, she'd reassured him and ruffled his hair in her usual way. He would be an uncle by this time tomorrow, she said, but for now, do go up to the field and find your brother. No, your mother – she would be of much greater help. And only then your brother, she laughed, as she shooed him out of the door.

Unlike his grandmother she had died at night, and certainly not quietly. He'd woken up to heavy footsteps, and later wailing, and his mother, red-faced, had screamed at him to go out to the barn and stay there. When he'd woken with the sunrise and looked up at the bedroom window, he felt a hand in his hair and knew his sister-in-law was dead. His brother lay alone on the bed, on clean sheets Sarah-Jane had washed just days before, and Matthew was to sleep in the barn until after the burial day.

It was another quarter of a mile to the next coffin stone, where they'd be able to rest the casket, and their legs. Suddenly, without warning, Matthew felt the men's slow but steady tempo come to an ungraceful halt. William, Sarah-Jane's father, had pulled up sharply but the others' reflexes hadn't been quite so quick. There was a wobble, a series of tiny adjustments, then stillness.

Matthew watched the dust settle around his brother's feet. The box felt heavier than ever.

Then, two things happened, almost at once. First, Matthew felt the coffin tip forward slightly, as his brother's knees buckled. He had to engage all the muscles in his arm to avoid a lethal tilting. A split second later he saw what looked like a streak of thick pipe smoke winding along the dusty path towards them. His breath held itself tightly, instinct told him to run, but the casket kept each man trapped firmly where he stood.

The adder was jet black, three feet long and well fed. Not only was it bigger than any Matthew had seen before, but it was much closer than they ever came. Teased out from the grasses onto the dry warmth of the path, it was sliding soundlessly towards Luke's boots. Despite the heat of the day, Matthew felt a bitter chill on his skin, his head dizzy and dazed, all energy sapped from his body. He closed his eyes and time seemed to stop, then with a rushing sound he felt his mind being yanked backwards to another day they'd taken this path together.

It had been a Sunday last May. Late morning sun had usurped light showers, but not before they'd wet the path and turned the quartz in the coffin stones to sparkles. Pipers and fiddlers led the way, followed by the bride and groom, then Matthew and his mother, arm in arm. After the wedding, they'd celebrated in the barn, Matthew wearing the waistcoat that had fit him then and dancing the old Celtic reels with his new sister-in-law. The following morning, he and Luke had rescued the delicate white flowers, fallen from the bouquet and from Sarah-Jane's hair, into the dirt. Luke had painstakingly washed them under the pump and placed them in their mother's best crystal vase. He'd taken them to Sarah-Jane in bed, announcing the first day of their married life, Matthew trailing shyly behind with the breakfast tray. Sarah-Jane had laughed and told her new husband he could bring her flowers every morning, so long as he didn't forget to collect the eggs first.

Breakfast in bed was too cumbersome to do often, but Luke's devotion hadn't faltered as the summer gave way to autumn. By the end of the year, the baby was on the way.

When Matthew opened his eyes, it was today again. The snake had stopped in front of his brother's feet and Luke was looking down at it, as still as a standing stone, knowing any sudden movement risked a strike. Matthew's fear rose now from his belly to his throat, then disappeared as his senses seemed to fail. The sounds of the shrieking gulls, and the kittiwakes, faded and were gone. He could no longer feel the weight of the coffin, nor the ache in his neck. Only his sight remained, and Matthew found he couldn't close his eyes as the snake began to move again, slithering closer to his brother's feet. Seized with terror now, he watched, eyes wide, as it languidly wound its way around Luke's boots, three times widdershins, coming to rest neatly in its starting place. It raised itself as if to strike, and Matthew saw his brother's head dip slightly, as if nodding solemnly to the serpent, before it streaked quickly away and seemed to vanish once more.

As if a spell had been broken, one by one Matthew felt his senses returning. The sweat on the back of his neck made him itch again, his throat was dry, the waistcoat was still too tight. Sarah-Jane's three brothers laughed nervously and with a shuffle the gloomy walk continued. At the final coffin stone before the church, they laid the casket down carefully, Sarah-Jane's brothers slapping their father's back and sitting gratefully next to it. Luke only stared, as if he could see his dead wife and child in the shine of the wood. Matthew pushed his hands flat on the cool granite and held them to his neck. The church bells rang already; the heat had slowed them down. He realised he had no sense of how long they'd stopped for. Indeed, the more he thought about it, the more he couldn't quite grasp the memory at all. He had a lingering sense of the snake, and that something important had happened, but could not for the life of him imagine what. Heat could play tricks on you, after all, and the others said nothing. He looked at his brother, but Luke looked away.

In the days following the funeral, no-one was quite sure who had been the last person to see Luke. Mrs Trembath thought she'd seen him, right after the burial, heading for the cove where he'd played as a child. She'd told his mother she'd thought that strange. But she was the oldest person in the parish, and half blind. The churchwarden was adamant he'd seen Luke in the late afternoon, staggering through the gorse towards nowhere. He'd called out loudly to him, to question why he wasn't bound for home, but Luke hadn't shown any sign he'd heard a thing. What was curious, the churchwarden thought, was that the young man had been fully clothed yet barefoot. If this was true, it would mean that the pair of boots he found sitting neatly on the coffin stone behind the church were almost certainly Luke's, but he had no explanation for why the lad would have gone for a walk without his shoes on.

As for the rest of the villagers – for the whole village had turned out for the service – they each found they couldn't quite pinpoint when they had last seen him. He'd certainly been there in the church, and they'd seen him outside afterwards, gazing at the casket being sunk into the ground. Some had tried to speak to him, for they were kind people and usually shared their sorrows, but he'd seemed preoccupied, and was mute. And then it had felt as though he was with them on the walk back up to the farm, but now, when you think about it, was he?

By the time the harvest was due to begin, the village was awash with rumours, and Matthew had heard them all. That his brother had been enticed into the ocean by a magnificent mermaid, the story varying from time to time as to the colour of the mermaid's hair and how willing his brother had been to join her. Another was that he had left the churchyard and simply walked the three hundred miles to London, no longer able to live on the farm where his wife had died, nor worship in the church where he had married and buried her. Some said he had walked not to

London but to Newlyn and boarded a ship sailing to the Americas from the Old Quay there. Some of the farm workers said they'd seen gypsies in the Steeple Woods, and that Luke had run away with them to live, roaming and rootless. He would be back, their wives said, but only as an old man.

All Mother would say was that it was utter nonsense. Luke had been a simple child, and a rational man, and he would have laughed at some of the more fanciful stories. He'd gone alright, and it was what it was. She'd sighed, and said no more. At Christmas, she didn't embroider a new handkerchief, nor set a place at the table. Matthew took over his brother's jobs on the farm, and in time, the gossip and speculation died away.

Matthew never told anyone, not even Mother, about the snake. Nor did he mention he'd thought he'd seen Luke himself, after the burial. Thinking his brother had returned to the farm, he'd stayed behind all afternoon at the graveside; he hadn't wanted to leave. When he eventually started the climb up the hill something had compelled him to turn and look back the way he came. Beyond the church he saw the sweep of the land and beyond that, he'd been told, England began. He heard frenzied seabirds, felt the sun prickling his neck and knew, although he was sad, he was rooted in the earth once more. The morning's weird events had surely been a delusion, a cruel daydream created by heat and lack of sleep. He felt, with great relief, that it was over.

As he'd made to leave, he saw the heavy wooden door of the church open and, to his surprise, his brother appear from the darkness. Matthew watched as Luke took the several steps across the grass towards the coffin path. Good, he thought, they would walk home together. But instead, Luke stopped at the coffin stone and sat on it carefully, back poker straight, hands caressing the rock. Matthew watched him lift his feet, one after the other, and gently untie each boot, sitting them neatly beside him on the stone. How peculiar, the boy thought, as Luke looked up at the cloudless sky. Then, this man he'd known all his life slowly lay back along the smooth granite, bare feet flat on the ground, as if waiting. I'll go to him, thought the boy, and bring him home.

From the undergrowth near Matthew's feet there came a gentle rustling. The dreadful black snake emerged, gliding soundlessly, blocking his path to the church. Again he felt his muscles seize, the strength drain at once from his body. Calmly, precisely, the creature's head rose from the dust. The boy saw the forked, flicking tongue, heard the eerie hiss of forewarning. Lidless eyes, copper-red, locked and held him. But astonishingly, it did not strike him. Instead, Matthew could only watch as it jack-knifed around and slithered eagerly down the path, toward the coffin stone.

Seized with terror now, he watched, eyes wide, as it languidly wound its way around Luke's boots, three times widdershins, coming to rest neatly in its starting place.

AUTHOR

C. M. Davis

The geography and landscape of a place shape and define its people. To me, living in West Penwith invokes a blurring of boundaries; communities occupying a liminal space between land and sea. Villages are bounded by a relentlessly pounding Atlantic on one side and rocky moorland, scattered with ancient standing stones, on the other. The coffin path is set in the early 19th Century, as I also wanted to embody the sense of isolation, and the closeness to nature, that was perhaps even more profound on the peninsula in those times. It is the ideal backdrop for a story which explores the delicate line between truth and interpretation.

NOW IS THE TIME FOR

US TO RISE FROM SLEEP

by Cathy Rentzenbrink
(Section 08 - South Coast Western)

She opens her eyes with a start, feels a chill on her arms, the stone under her back. Where is she? She pulls herself up. It is getting too dark to see. She can make out the shapes of bushes and trees but not much more. She pats her hands around her, finds the edges of the stone. Remembers. She is on the pilgrim's ledge.

Her heart quickens. Almost she can hear the thud of it over the sound of the sea washing against the side of the mount. A low hoot comes from the wood. The lights of Penzance twinkle far across the bay. It is not far back to the flat. A few minutes. But how will she find her way? Too dangerous, surely, to go blundering around, arms stretched out into the darkness.

She shouldn't have stayed out this late. Not that it was part of the plan. She didn't mean to go to sleep, just do a little exploring. She'd wanted to soak up the atmosphere, to try to think herself into the mind of a monk in medieval times. For a story, of course. Everything she does these days is in the service of her writing. Sometimes that feels like a privilege. Sometimes she feels like a maggot munching her way through the flesh of life so she can regurgitate it into words as fast as she can.

'How important is writing to you?' someone asked her recently, at an event. 'It's everything,' she'd said, and then, 'But don't tell that to my family,' and the audience laughed, leaving her unsure as to whether she had been joking.

She does take it seriously and she puts in the hard yards. She considered the physicality of her mission, before setting off from the little flat above the cafe to climb the hill towards the castle. She'd changed into a linen dress because it was the nearest thing she owned to a habit. A shame it was bright blue – cornflower blue, according to the shop – rather than a more monastic brown, but the feel of it against her skin, she thought, would be the nearest she could get to the real thing. And she wore her flip-flops rather than her more substantial trainers because monks wouldn't have had trainers, would they? And she left her phone in the flat because the consciousness she is trying to think herself into would not have known the continual connection that is the luxury and burden of the twenty-first century. Her glasses, too. She'd weighed up the pros and cons, taken them off, put them back on again, looked out of the window with and without, and then decided in favour of authenticity. Monks would definitely not have had varifocals. But she knew she would have to be careful; she would feel silly if she twisted an ankle in pursuit of her writerly goals. Or worse. Tumbled off the side of the mount, dunked herself into the sea. How novelistic! Not that this is much better. She feels foolish and naughty. What a thing to fall asleep. Perhaps she would earn a few paragraphs in the paper. She imagines people sniggering over her stupidity as they eat their breakfast: 'This writer went out in flip-flops to try to think like a monk, fell asleep and then got lost in the dark and then drowned in the sea.' No, she doesn't want that.

Presumably they didn't come down here in the dark, the monks. Unless there was a moon. Would they have any kind of spectacles? Some kind of magnifier, perhaps. She doesn't know. That's part of the problem with this story she is writing. She doesn't know enough about the daily life of the person she is trying to conjure. Is it difficult to walk in someone else's shoes when she can't even imagine how they would feel on her feet. Though it is mainly a question of stripping back, she thinks, trying to forget all the information that sloshes around in her head, so she can slip out from under the leash of contemporary life. She finds it hard enough these days to remember what life was like without a smartphone, let alone drift further back through the centuries, before Galileo, before people understood about the Earth and the sun, and that day would always follow night. Before trains and newspapers and electricity. Before battery-powered torches. She imagines the monks lived by the rhythms of the natural light, though she knows from her research that they did have to get up in the dark for more prayer – the night office – before going back to bed again – a pallet? – until daybreak and Lauds.

She has been reading The Rule of St Benedict, a practical guide to monastic life. It felt attractive to her at first. She was on a plane to a literary festival in Belfast and thought there could be something calming and wholesome about living on a strict schedule for prayer, manual labour, and lectio divina, the rather beautiful expression for spiritual reading. But then the more she read about the need for humility and obedience, she thought it would not suit her at all. She has never liked being told what to do. She could live with not having personal belongings – she's never been bothered about stuff – but not without personal relationships. Imagine not being allowed to talk to anyone who has been deemed deserving of punishment. And St Benedict is big on the sin of pride, discouraging monks even from taking any satisfaction in reading aloud too well to the other monks. A memory comes unbidden. She went to a Catholic school, because it was the nearest, and read in Mass because she was good at it. Once one of the teachers complained that her red headband was too bright, that she needed to be more restrained, to cultivate an air of modesty. And there was that time another teacher told her off for knocking too confidently on the staffroom door.

She shifts herself around, sits cross-legged. Her ankle bone frets against the stone. If she was more disciplined about doing yoga, then she'd find this easier. She looks out into the dark. Is she really going to stay here all night? There is another option. She could scream and shout. The island is not big. If she made enough noise, she might attract the attention of a rescuer who could bring light and show her the way back to the path and to her soft bed. But how embarrassing! If she were in danger of her life, she might be able to bring herself to make a fuss but not to avoid a bit of discomfort. She can't think she is in any actual peril. The ledge does stick out a bit, she'd better try to avoid rolling off it, but it wouldn't be the end of the world if she did. Just a bit of pain and humiliation. St Benedict would probably think it would be good for her.

She resigns herself to her situation, accepts that she will stay on the ledge until dawn. Counts her blessings. There has been a heatwave for days, and luckily she is wearing a pair of leggings, not because she needed them for warmth earlier, but because she dislikes displaying her legs, which are so white they are almost purple. And the nights don't last that long at this time of year. It will be a handful of hours only until the sun rises and she can see her way back to the flat. She has already eaten so she is not hungry. She is not having her period. She is not missing anything or letting anyone down. She might get a bit cold as she goes deeper into night, but she'll survive.

All she had meant to do was close her eyes for a few moments, the better to appreciate the sounds of the island. The soundscape, as she'd heard it described on the radio recently. She had hoped to connect to her fictional monk by sharing an aural experience with him. She's been getting more into her senses lately, as she has been trying to be more mindful. She did it in her workshop earlier, got her writers – all competition winners from sixth form colleges throughout Cornwall – to close their eyes for five minutes and concentrate on all their other senses. They seemed to like it. At least none of them dropped off, which can happen when the group demographic is older.

So she decided to try it for herself. It had been pointed out to her, this place, on the tour she was given when she arrived. The pilgrim's ledge. No-one really knows what it was used for, but it is easy to imagine that the monks would have come here singly to commune with God. There is only really room for one person. A slab of stone set back in the cliff. Not quite a cave but sheltered from the elements. She had sat down in the warmth of the setting sun and then had stretched out, enjoying the sensation of the hard surface against her back. Maybe they did this, the monks, she thought, maybe they lay and soaked up the sun and released their troubles into the ground. And then she must have gone to sleep.

Because she is tired, of course. So tired from criss-crossing the country. Belfast and Orkney and Guernsey and Bradford all in the last couple of weeks. That would have fucked St Benedict right up, trying to observe the rule while on the road. She is healthy at home but is always living off Mars bars and flapjacks when travelling around. Pizza slices. Naan chips dipped in hummus. The best brownies in the world. Hotel room biscuits. And she never knows when she'll be eating roast pheasant from a golden plate or be abandoned after hours on a train in a B & B miles from anywhere with a grumpy landlady who grudgingly rustles up a cup of tea and two custard creams. She's had excruciating experiences, sometimes.

She's learnt to nod and smile while audience members critique the elements of her life she's shared in her books. And people do press religion on her, offer her God as the answer to all her problems. She's used to that though, has come to find it rather sweet. And she does love the talking to strangers. She takes a pride that St Benedict would consider ungodly in doing her events, her readings, in connecting with her fellow humans. If only life could be like a creative writing workshop, if she could do this non-stop, she'd thought earlier, as she'd talked the group through the exercises she'd created based on the history and legends of the island. She'd got them to imagine they were one of the fishermen who had first seen St Michael appear. Then to write a scene from the perspective of Sir John St Aubyn, an abolitionist who was also a notorious womaniser and gambler. He fell out with his friend and neighbour Sir Francis Basset, but their portraits now hang together. She asked the group to write the quarrel. What might they have argued about? And she had them trying to solve the mystery of the bones of the giant man discovered in a tiny room under the church. What was he doing there? There are various theories, the guide had told her, and pointed out that the man got an inch taller every time there was another news item about him. His bones used to be displayed but now he has been given his privacy and is interred in an unmarked grave. And she told the students her idea for a story about a young monk, given to the church in infancy. A boy who craves touch and affection and something other than divine love and who thinks, therefore, is told, that he is sinful. Most people believed in God then, she explained, and thought that he could see into their disobedient hearts. St Benedict warned that death lies at the gateway to pleasure. Imagine what it would be like to believe that your desires meant you were rotten, corrupt, and in thrall to the devil.

She shivers. Maybe monks were brought down here to spend the night repenting. Perhaps the abbot would say, 'A night on the ledge for you,' and they would sit as she is, thinking and remembering and trying not to be freaked out by the rustlings in the woods. The owls sound companionable, almost like they are whispering secrets. Though, with no human beings to take it upon themselves to accuse them of sin, they probably are lacking in shame, and therefore don't have anything to feel bad about.

It is such hard work being a human. And now, too, in

this world where technology means that everyone knows everything but loses sight of what matters. You don't have to be a theologist to clock the connection between the plagues and the floods and the possibility of the end of it all. She rubs her hands over her arms. It is getting colder. She needs to think of something more cheerful.

She lies down on the stone, stretches out and then curls up. She puts her hands together and pillows them under her cheek. She can't say she is comfortable. How long until dawn? Four or five hours? She does what she has trained herself to do last thing every night and plays a slideshow of the nice things that happened that day. She sees herself on the train, looking out at the mount as she pulled into Penzance station, the friendly young man who picked her up, the boat trip across the bay, the feel of the spray on her face, the taste of the salt in the air, the tour of the island, texting her son photographs of the giant's heart and the giant's well, settling into the flat, teaching her workshop in the refectory where the monks would have eaten, the eager and innocent faces of her students, that feeling that she has found a place where she is meant to be, a way to be useful, the calm certainty that comes over her at the rightness of encouraging others to write, of being in service to their creativity.

She wakes. The birds are singing. She keeps her eyes closed for a moment, the better to hear. She can hardly even find words to describe the sounds. Caws, cries, shrieks, tweets, chirps. A cacophony. The dawn chorus. She knows the phrase, of course, but has never experienced it like this before. She opens her eyes, sits up. The sky is illuminated by the sun breaking behind the mount. Blues, greys, pinks. It is the most beautiful thing she has ever seen. She unfolds herself. Her body is stiff from the night on the floor, but her mind feels fresh and clean.

She swings her legs over the side of the ledge. It is a good job she didn't roll off. There is a bit of a drop. But she didn't. She kept herself safe, or was kept safe, so that she could experience this morning. Penzance looks further away than it did in the dark. She feels like there is only this, that only her immediate surroundings matter. Trees, bushes, grass. They are not only green but so green, so many different shades. She could stay here forever and not count them all. And the flowers. Flashes of pink and yellow. And the sea! What magnificence. A moving, glittering, glory of blues.

And she gets a glimpse of what life was like all those centuries ago, when the dark of each night felt like it might last forever, when the sunrise everyday was experienced as a blessed relief. Yes, it would feel divine, this, if she didn't know what she knows about the Earth's orbit. The cornflower blue of her crumpled tunic looks as bright as the colour of heaven. She eases herself onto her knees. She does want to give thanks for this morning. She sees a boat heading out across the bay. Fishermen? Maybe if she stood, they might catch sight of her and take her for a holy saint. It occurs to her that she is not wearing her glasses, but that she has never seen so well, never been so aware of all the colour in this world, so alive to the possibilities of her senses. A night off screens, perhaps, away from the noise and clamour, but she resists the attempts of her mind to provide rational explanation. She feels the stone under her knees, closes her eyes and opens them again. Maybe she can choose to feel this morning, to experience it without thinking, without trying to corral it into language, perhaps she can just take some more moments to be with this dawn, this feeling of gratitude and awe that the sun has risen again and that both she and the Earth have been gifted another day.

And he arrives then, the character she has been looking for. He walks out of the dawn in a habit and sandals. He is scarcely more than a boy. He looks troubled, his head bowed. He has known nothing but this island and the rule of his abbot. He wants to touch and be touched. But he knows that what he wants is wrong. God sees all his actions and knows his thoughts and death lies at the gateway of pleasure.

So when he looks at the profile of one of the other boys at prayers and aches to stretch out his fingers and stroke his cheek, he believes that the Devil is inside him, blackening his heart and his soul. Yes, she sees him clearly, there through the early morning mist, looking out to sea, holding his trembling fingers together. He is praying for his sins to be forgiven, for the burn of lust to cool, to be able to withstand temptation, but – all at the same time, hardly even aware of it – he has a sense that there could be a different way. Maybe there is another time and place where his desires do not make him dirty and wrong and where he does not have to choose between divine and earthly love. Perhaps there is a possibility for him beyond sin and suffering.

And she leans back and watches him look out to sea and considers how she can help him to plot his escape.

And he arrives then, the character she has been looking for. He walks out of the dawn in a habit and sandals. He is scarcely more than a boy. He looks troubled, his head bowed.

AUTHOR

Cathy Rentzenbrink

I first encountered St Michael's Mount as a picture on a china plate owned by my granny. A castle surrounded by sea, it looked like something from Narnia and it still holds a place in my imaginative affection that doesn't feel fully real. When I go there now, my feet may be in the 21st century but part of me knows that the right step, or a squint of my eyes, could transport me back in time. The gift shop will vanish, and the chatter of the guests over their cream teas will be replaced with the whispering of monks on their way to Vespers. The magic endures.

LONE CYPRESS

by Philip Marsden
(Section 09 - South Coast Central)

Strange how it affects you. More than something that has simply broken. More than a cup or a favourite vase, different from the death of a calf or horse or dog. One day upright and the next on its side, roots probing the air, the earth beneath it ripped open and wounded, a towering thing fallen – time toppled, permanence upended.

None of these things occurred to Rachel when she first saw the tree in the dawn light. She had risen to open the curtains and – oof! So, that was the noise, the roar and hiss she'd half-heard through her sleep. Now she simply thought: it has missed the buildings and the old piggery and the barn; it has missed the red Devons – there they are, sheltering beneath the trees. It has not missed the wall beside the drive and it'll all need to be cleared. And then, because it was still on her mind and because however far she roamed in her thinking she always returned – Dad, he's been spared this.

All morning the chainsaw wailed. Ivan had come when she phoned him and he saw what needed doing and got on with doing it, as he always did. She walked round the yard with the dogs, checking for damage, tending to the silage pit where the wind had lifted a length of black plastic and shifted the tractor tyres, and a tarpaulin that had come loose. She checked the slates on the outbuildings, made a pile of dead branches that lay scattered beneath the ashes.

She then crossed the field and leaned her forearms on the top gate. The wind had eased a little and the sky was clear. Freshness flowed around her, as if it was not a bad thing that had happened overnight but a cleansing. In the pasture ahead, new-growth May grass was pressed flat. Hawthorn flowers were scattered over it. She looked out beyond the lane, beyond the treetops in the steep valley. She could see the sea breaking white on the Dodman point, some three miles off and she did that thing she always did here as a child – closing her eyes, imagining the view as a bird would see it, flying over the cliff and out across the open water.

Just a week now since the funeral – that strange assembly of whispering figures in Veryan church. Faces from the old days transformed by the years, age-worn hands taking the service sheets, stepping into the stone interior and its hesitant fluting organ. All day she'd felt like a stranger. It was someone else's funeral, someone else's Dad. Then the coffin was carried to the plot beneath the trees, with the family headstones around it, going back through the 1800s and the newest one with Mum's dates, Mum's name and maiden name.

Now it was just her and the weight of all those behind, and the farm. If she'd thought ahead, she would have seen it coming. But thinking ahead was never her thing. After all the years away, she didn't think twice about coming home when Dad was ill. Compassionate leave to begin with, and when the days became weeks and months, she found it easy to hand in her notice and give up the rent on the flat. The truth was that she liked it here. She liked the familiarity of home. Looking after Dad gave her more purpose than pushing papers at the Nightingale Hospital in Exeter. When her friends came to visit on her birthday, they'd said how well she looked. The rhythms of the farm made her happy. But something was nagging at that happiness, telling her it was not the place she should be.

In the parish hall after the service, everyone came up and tried to say the right thing. Only Mary Trevail came straight out with it. 'Will you be staying then, taking on the farm?'

Rachel knew what she was really saying: 'You're not going to flit off and betray us, abandon everything your family ever worked for?'

The chainsaw again, in the distance. Coming round

the front of the house, Rachel saw swifts, three of them, spinning round the roof and the gables where they nested. They appeared oblivious to the fallen hulk of the tree. They'd only been back a few days. Thousands of miles from Africa and they knew exactly where to come, and exactly when. They arrived every year within a day or two of 10 May. Oh, for such certainty, such a lack of choice!

She stopped before the fallen tree. It was hard to think of the farm without it. When she conjured up home, it was here of course, Cornwall, the lanes and the cliffs and the wooded valleys of the Roseland. But the picture in her mind was the front of the house – the neat little porch and the dark green, evergreen mass of macrocarpus foliage. As it had grown, the tree had slowly covered the house, shunting it to the shadows.

She ran her fingers over the lines in the bark. They ran in intersecting curves, but now sideways and not up-and-down as they always had, rising like flame into the spreading canopy. It was wrong that something so big should collapse – against the natural order of things. And from somewhere inside her came a fear so vast that on that May morning she found herself shivering.

'You wouldn't leave, would you?'

He'd only asked her directly once, shortly after Mum died, when he first became seriously ill.

'Of course not. I'm here now.'

It was what he wanted to hear, and what she wanted to tell him. And she believed it at the time. Mum and Dad had always been there, and even when it became clear they would not be, when she'd come back to look after Dad, she'd always had more immediate things to think about – his illness, the day-to-day running of the farm, the funeral.

Now there was no avoiding it. Sell up or stay.

She went inside and slid the kettle onto the hot plate. The brightness in the kitchen was something new, as if there was snow outside. Mum had always complained of the light it took, and then Dad would lop off a bough or two, to keep her happy. Once she said to him: 'It has grown too big, shouldn't we take it down?' Rachel remembered his look then. Not defiance or anger, just confusion.

A pile of papers lay on the table – letters in Dad's name, invoices from feed suppliers, from Vincent Tractors, notes of condolence. She sorted them into piles, again, squared them off neatly, then took one at random. It was a valuation form, asking her for an inventory of farm equipment, and for the signed agreement. What signed agreement?

She looked out the window. She raised the mug to her lips. She inspected her nails. Then, firmly, she pushed the papers to one side, raised the lid on her laptop and googled 'macrocarpa'.

Cupressus macrocarpa – the Monterey Cypress. The tree came originally from California, from the Monterey peninsula. The macrocarpa there were 'relicts'. They were survivors of an ancient forest that was believed to have dominated that part of North America during the last

Ice Age. Over time, they had become fewer. Now they were very rare – confined to just two sites. But people had taken seeds up the coast to Oregon, to New Zealand and Australia, and to France and Ireland and Britain. In hotter places it had proved susceptible to canker and fungus; in its native California it was badly affected. But it liked rain and thrived in a cooler climate – hence Cornwall.

'The Monterey Cypress,' she read, 'grows bigger and better in its non-native places.'

And it came to her again – her own question: better to stay or leave?

From the cupboard by the window, she retrieved the old photo albums. It was an age since she'd looked at them. She found her twenty-first birthday party – just eight years ago, but already it was another era. The next-morning group in front of the house, around the tree – there was LB and Sam and some of the St Mawes boys who had climbed into the lower branches and were looning about. Then, some years earlier – her with a pony tail and the coat with horses on it, standing beside the macrocarpa, with that fierce-looking woman. Who was that? And here's that round-cheeked and plump toddler in a romper suit with Mum and snow on the ground and on the roof. The tree was barely up to the top of the windows.

She knew all these pictures. They were like old songs. All the faces came back to her, if not the names. Now she found herself looking not at the people but at the tree. She turned a page and there were Mum and Dad, before she was born, young and smooth-faced, about the age she was now. The tree was between them, barely up to their waist, like the child they did not yet have.

She remembered Mum saying they'd planted the tree as soon as they moved in, when Gran and Granfer had gone to the cottage. And she remembered how surprised they always were with the speed of its growth.

In the coming days, Ivan chopped up the tree and made a pile of the brush. The daily business of the farm continued; the question remained. 'The Monterey Cypress grows bigger and better in its non-native places' – she was haunted by that, and also by the picture she'd seen at the same time. It was one of the few macrocarpa left in Monterey. It appeared to be growing out of a lump of bare rock, with the sea stretching beyond it. Known as 'the Lone Cypress', it had appeared on numerous postcards over the years. It was said to be the 'most photographed tree in the world'. But it couldn't stand up on its own any longer. It was held in place by wires. In 2019, a large bough had fallen off. No-one was quite sure how long the rest would last.

May again, and Rachel was exhausted. She had cleared the house and the attic, all the cupboards and wardrobes. The barns were empty and three skip-loads of old junk, unused tools and equipment, had been taken away. The herd had been sold to a farm near Wadebridge and all the machinery, tractors and trailers had gone at auction.

A man from Wiltshire bought the farm itself – not a

farmer, but he wanted the land. He wasn't going to live here full-time and would let out most of the good fields; the rest would be planted with trees and rewilded. Dad would have hated that, waste of good farmland.

She had put down the deposit on a house in Exeter. She had money now; she wouldn't go back to her old job. She wanted to train as a nurse. Although it was all appealing in its way – it was where her friends were, the place she knew – she felt less pulled there than pushed. In the end, she was more afraid of staying than leaving.

Her old school friends, those who'd remained and married, had expressed nothing but sadness. Old Mary Trevail had appeared to soften: 'It's a lot to take on, on your own. Your mother and father always knew that.' She didn't need to say out loud what Rachel knew she was really thinking: 'You've given in, you've taken the money – another farm gone, another Cornish family wiped away.'

The tree had been chopped up and split. All last winter – that strange and lonely winter when she'd lived as an imposter in the house – Rachel had been burning the wood in the stoves. She became familiar with the sweet smell and the spitty logs. She was amazed how fast the wood-pile diminished, how fast the tree just disappeared.

Ivan was staying on. 'I'll do whatever he wants. I don't really mind.' She knew he loved the land; in a rare sense, it was him who it belonged to. Last week, he'd handed her a cardboard box, with his shy smile. She lifted the lid. It was a wooden bowl – a deep orange-brown fruit bowl, polished and oiled. 'Came from down near the base. Look – there's a lovely twist in the grain. I turned it myself.'

On the last morning, the furniture vans came early. She let them get on with it. She walked out beyond the empty barns and the empty yard and crossed the empty paddock. With the cattle gone, there was a stillness about everything. She stood at the gate and looked out to the Dodman. There were white-caps on the water below, and a white sail and then just the flat infinity of the horizon.

Returning by the top fields, she looked down on the house. Porch, windows, stonework, as it always had been – everything but the great green canopy of the tree. It was then that she felt the tears rise – and they kept on coming, from some deep well-spring of grief that she hadn't yet accessed: grief for the farm and the herd, grief for Mum and Dad, all they'd done here over the years, all they'd done for her and how she'd never thought to thank them, grief for herself and the time that had passed here, and nothing now, no longer home, nothing but a void – and the tears kept coming.

By the time she reached the house, her eyes had dried. The vans were filling up, boxes and bubble-wrapped tables and chairs standing outside in the sun and the tailgates of the lorries down. Overhead came the screech of the swifts and she looked up to watch two of them come dipping in past the gables, and spin away on those never-tiring wings. They would still be here after she'd gone and they would come back next year, and the next.

In front of the sitting-room window was the place where they'd dug out the stump. She'd only seeded it a month ago, and the grass had already begun to show.

By the end of the summer, the patch would have merged into the lawn, and then there'd be nothing left at all.

Coming round the front of the house, Rachel saw swifts, three of them, spinning round the roof and the gables where they nested. They appeared oblivious to the fallen hulk of the tree.

AUTHOR

Philip Marsden

Macrocarpa trees are a feature of the Cornish landscape – a great many were planted semi-ornamentally in the early-mid-twentieth century. They are magnificent trees, but shallow-rooted.

After a winter storm a couple of years ago, there was a video online of one toppling over in Bude. We had two at my own farm on the Roseland, but they were beginning to move in gales, and because they were immediately up-wind of my neighbour's house, they had to come down.

Trees are a bit like teeth: their loss reminds us of our own mortality and familiar views look a bit strange without them. In the story, the tree stands for the deceptive solidity of home, and roots being shallower than we think.

THE INCIDENTS

by Wyl Menmuir
(Section 10 - South Coast Eastern)

After it happened the first time, Blue Adderleigh's mother had laughed. It was a shaky laugh. A we-dodged-a-bullet-there laugh. Over the next few days, though, the laugh evolved into one that felt like the kind that would be appropriate to accompany an after-dinner story.

If I hadn't seen it, I wouldn't have believed it either, Emmaline Adderleigh said to her assembled guests the following week, employing said laugh. It's not something I'll forget in a hurry.

The story went that the proud parents had been out walking their new charge and stopped at The Green Man at Hurst for a light lunch, leaving the child asleep in the pram outside. They emerged some two hours later to find a crowd of locals gathered around a pram that looked very much like theirs, only this one was filled entirely with bees, as though someone had turned on a hose and filled the basket to the brim with them. At first, she and her husband had joined the gawping crowd, amazed at the spectacle of it, though when they looked for the pram with their child in it, they could not see it anywhere and it dawned on them that this was their pram and that their daughter was, most likely, buried somewhere deep within the darkly buzzing swarm that had, until just then, held only fascination for them.

Emmaline shouted for her husband to do something about it and – this featured in the story, too – he called for a gun with which to scare the bees off, so it was left to Emmaline to call for someone, anyone, to stop standing around staring and find a damned beekeeper.

Messengers were dispatched in search of the beekeeper and a barman took charge of the gun that Thomas Adderleigh had requisitioned, though which he had not yet managed to discharge. A short while later the village beekeeper arrived, an elderly man who calmly set about searching for the hairless queen, while Emmaline screamed, and Thomas demanded that he should be given the gun back in case the beekeeper failed. The gun was never needed, as the beekeeper eventually located the queen at the very heart of the swarm, tucked in one of the baby's palms. As he drew the bees away, carrying the queen aloft, it became clear that the child was unharmed and, further, that she was still asleep. The only sign that anything had happened was the gentle opening and closing of the hand in which Blue had held the queen, as though she was searching for it again in the midst of her dream.

The Adderleighs resolved to keep a closer eye on Blue after that. And though the story of the bees drew the best response from the room, Emmaline stopped telling it at some point around the second of what she began to refer to as 'the incidents'. Blue was toddling by this point and had taken to exploring the gardens. One morning in early summer, while her parents sat on reclining chairs on the lawn beneath parasols, reading impractically large newspapers, she wandered off the manicured lawns into the rough. When she emerged, her legs and dress green with grass slicks, she held in one of her hands the neck of a mottled snake perhaps twenty inches long. She proceeded to wrap it around her neck as though it was one of her mother's winter stoles. Again, her father called loudly for a gun and Emmaline screamed at the sight of a snake so close to the house. Eventually, after Blue had twirled on the lawn with the snake for a while as she had seen her mother do with scarves in front of the mirror, it dropped to the ground and returned to the rough.

Later that evening, her father, having rehearsed the story in his head all afternoon, told it over dinner and was surprised when Emmaline stood abruptly, upsetting her plate, and snapped at him – Jesus, Thomas, could you show some goddam sensitivity – and left him to deal with their guests without any clue as to what he had done wrong.

The stories of Blue's way with animals – or, rather, their way with her – were shelved and the other incidents were not spoken of at all, not even between Emmaline and Thomas. They did not discuss her near smothering by a clowder of cats that appeared one morning like a sudden plague and that disappeared so quickly it was difficult to imagine they had been there at all. Nor the fledgling that Emmaline discovered nesting in her daughter's hair and which had, by the advanced state of the nest, clearly been there for some time. Nor, in the last light of day, the deer that had emerged from the woods behind the house and which leapt directly over the child, the fur of its brush grazing the top of her head.

Eventually though, Emmaline took Blue to a psychotherapist who was unable to uncover the root trauma that had led to these events occurring. He was, however, glad of the business and suggested they should continue with the sessions until this trauma surfaced which he said it would, inevitably, given time.

In the winter of Blue's fifteenth year, Thomas Adderleigh died. It was an unremarkable death and did not make a good story. With her newfound freedom Emmaline bought a motorcar, the first she had owned. In a rare show of parental engagement, she asked Blue to choose the location of the holiday they would take in it and Blue chose the town of Fowey in Cornwall, where she dreamt of making the acquaintance of Daphne du Maurier, whose stories she admired and who she regularly imagined meeting, in passing and to the genuine delight of both parties. She was sure they would fall into a kind of easy conversation that would result in an invitation to stay, would later grow to correspondence, and from there to an inevitable and lifelong friendship.

Blue was surprised when her mother agreed to the suggestion. Her mother considered du Maurier's books to be little more than potboilers. Emmaline had friends in the area, though, and wrote to arrange to visit at their large house nearby at Lansallos, where they were – Emmaline was assured – awaited with concern and sympathy for their loss. On the long car journey west, Blue's mother described their host, David Moat, as a friend from college, though it was clear even then that there was more to it than that. When Blue pressed her mother for details, she changed the subject to the various rules she was imposing on her daughter for the visit. Blue was, firstly, not to ask the Moats if they were acquainted with Ms du Maurier nor, if it came up in conversation that they were, was she to ask for an introduction under any circumstances. She was not to encourage the attention of any animals nor make a nuisance of herself in any way. Neither was she to encourage the attention of the two Moat sons, whatever that meant and no, Emmaline did not want to go into any further detail on that and would Blue desist from calling her 'Mother', it made her sound old.

The Moat house sat in a dip in the rolling hills, just out of sight of the sea, and on arrival David Moat announced that once the pair had settled in they would walk to the beach, where he had arranged a picnic. His wife would not be joining them, he explained, though his sons would. Blue tried to make conversation with the Moat boys though they seemed incapable of it, and instead shared indecipherable glances with one another and snickered each time she spoke to them. David strode along ahead of the group, down the driveway and out through the gates, acting the tour guide, and before they left the village he paused at the gate of the church. The Moats were responsible for the upkeep of the chancel, he said proprietorially, as though this explained everything, and Blue's mother nodded, clearly impressed. And here, in this very graveyard, were the graves of two notorious smugglers. He gestured to two thin gravestones, the writing on which could have said anything really, before sweeping Emmaline into the church. Blue held back and wandered in the churchyard though, after a while, she grew bored of the sensation of the two boys' eyes on her from between the gravestones, and she retreated into the church.

They are beautiful, are they not? Fifteenth century, David Moat was saying. He was waving his cigarette in the direction of the carvings on the pews. I offered to buy them, money in the church's pocket and all that, though no joy.

How ungrateful, she heard her mother murmur.

The couple, for that is what they seemed to Blue, wafted around the church. David's cigarette smoke and his loud, and not always terribly well-informed, opinions filled the small chapel. Blue knelt at one of the carved pew ends. The wood was dark and shone dully but as her eyes grew accustomed to the darkness, she made out griffins and flowers, snakes, cats and bees and, on the end of one, a carved face or, rather, three carved faces on the same head. One face looked forward and the other two, each of which shared one of the eyes of the first, looked out to either side. The faces were fringed with foliage which seemed to emerge from their mouths, making them beards of greenery, and their hair, too, was leaflike. The faces were serious and peaceful, or maybe disturbing, she couldn't tell which. Inscrutable would be the better word, perhaps, she thought. They had the features of men but they seemed to her more like the faces of animals. Though the eyes on all three faces were closed she imagined these figures were looking at her or, rather, seeing her across the centuries.

When she looked up again, the church was silent. David's monologue had ceased and she could tell by the settling of dust motes in the air, lit by shafts of light through the stained glass, that they had left the building and she had drifted. She could stay here for a while, in the dark and the cool, she thought. Though, as she was thinking this, from somewhere far away she heard her mother's voice shrilling. She rose, and before she left she stooped and touched the tip of an index finger to the forehead of the carved figure that faced outward from the bench.

The Moats were waiting for her on the road, impatient and hot. Emmaline gave her that look, the one she knew was meant to remind her of the instructions she had given in the car. Beyond the church they left the road, stepping over a stile through trees and suddenly there was the ocean, unrealistically blue against the green of the fields that folded down towards it. David Moat, leaning against a gate, pointed out a shack in the distance, built there, he said, by customs men to stem the flow of smuggled goods. It was owned by a writer now, he said. It was the shed from which she penned books for which he didn't have much time himself.

The sun was hot on their backs now, and David announced that it would be cooler on the valley path, under the trees. If anything though, it was hotter beneath the thick canopy. The greens seemed to Blue oppressively bright, and everything felt sharpened by the sensation of sweat pooling on her neck and dripping down her back.

The Moat boys were barking now, pushing and butting up against each other, and Blue was glad when they emerged from the tree tunnel and the sea came back into view and she felt the faintest of breezes as they crossed the last of the fields before the beach. There were birds on the cliffs and standing around on the grass too, a huge host of large white gulls that did not move as the party approached and through which they had to pick their way. The gulls seemed unperturbed when the Moat boys kicked at them. Blue could see intricate towers of orchids in the grass, though David was back onto the subject of smugglers and Blue did not feel she could interrupt to share this. Down there, David was saying, was where they'd drag the kegs off the beach, up through the cut they dug out of the rock. He did not approve of smugglers, of course. Thieves were thieves, though there was a certain thrill to the idea of getting one past the taxman who, after all, was just another sort of thief. They stepped down into the cleft and as they came out onto the beach Emmaline made a show of gasping at the wicker baskets and blankets set out on the sand. The Moat boys snickered at her and punched each other in the ribs.

Emmaline and David sat by one of the baskets and Blue, who was used to sitting at the children's table, even as an only child, sat by the other, which was some way off, kicking off her shoes as she settled on the blanket. The Moat boys did not sit, but stripped to their waists, not far from Blue's blanket, and fell to wrestling behind her. Blue took a sandwich from the basket and her book from her satchel and tried to ignore the flying sand and the boys' grunts and exertions.

The first gull that swooped in missed Blue's head by centimetres, though she felt its wings against her face as it flew over her shoulder, after her sandwich. The second one that dived in caught a crust and ripped a chunk out of it and by the time she had gathered her thoughts, the first had wheeled round and dived again, this time more successfully. Blue looked round to see if anyone was going to come to her rescue but the boys were entangled with one another – the arms and legs of one folded around those of the other in a complex knot. If I let you go, you've got to promise not to hurt me, right? one was saying to the other, somewhat breathlessly.

Behind Blue, Emmaline was laughing at some story of David's. Bothered more by the fighting and the flirting than the birds, Blue lifted the lid of the hamper and spread out the remaining sandwiches for the gulls. She rose and walked down to the shoreline, to the mica green sea, and paddled her feet. The water was cool and fresh and welcome and she waded in a little deeper. There were small fish in the shallows that gathered to her and brushed against her ankles and which, when she took a couple more steps, nibbled and tugged gently at the hem of her dress. She could see there were larger fish, too, just further out in the darker, deeper blue, waiting for her, starfish and mackerel and pipefish and sunfish in huge numbers, gathered there for her. She waded in further still, the small fish and the larger ones now circling her feet and calves, urging her on, and as she waded deeper still, her dress floating up around her, she could sense, in the waters beyond, the ponderous whales whose deep reverberations, she felt, called to her among those of the profound multitudes of the deep and their calls sounded like home.

The boys on the beach finished their wrestling, though by the time they wore themselves out and fell into a wary truce, they had forgotten what they were fighting about. They shooed off the gulls which had, by then, eaten what remained of the picnic. They were arguing again as they left the beach, about who had left the hamper open, and David and Emmaline were laughing at a joke they had first shared some twenty years earlier.

She rose, and before she left she stooped and touched the tip of an index finger to the forehead of the carved figure that faced outward from the bench.

AUTHOR

Wyl Menmuir

Fowey and the areas surrounding it are incredibly rich in terms of landscapes, from rolling hills, to dramatic cliffs, smugglers' cut-throughs, rolling hills and lush woodlands. It's a landscape of abundant possibilities, though one I knew better from seeing it from the sea rather than from land, and it was pure pleasure to walk - and draw inspiration from - the cliffs, woodlands, meadows and beaches here. The challenge was what to exclude rather than what to write in a place of abundant inspiration, so this story references folk tales, smugglers, Daphne du Maurier, and a walk I took at Lansallos.

THE BLACK PRINCE

by Edward Rowe
(Section 11 - Rame Head)

My mother, Sarah, with her eyesight failing and blindness lurking, gazes at family photos, moving them back and forth like a trombone. Sometimes a family member is touching her nose, and other times they're at full arm's length and she squints and frowns at them like she's trying to work out how on earth they are or were related. I imagine the classic trombone comedy sound effect at the end of a rubbish joke each time a picture moves away from her eyes and back again.

Wah wah wah waaah.

With her chin jutting, not only does she look baffled, but she also looks like she's firing lasers from her eyes at a particularly obscure relative.

I ask her who she's looking at. Mother, she says. Picture with me when I was six or seven.

Ah, Granny. Dear of her, I say.

I know what Mum is doing – she's etching the faces of our family into her mind before she loses her sight. I know what you're doing, I say, but she won't admit it and she ignores me. Mum, I say, I know what you're doing. She squints at me and juts her jaw and I feel the lasers burn into my body.

Tea? I ask.

Do you hear that? That's the band starting up. Won't be too long now. Last one for this old maid!

Don't be silly. It won't be your last, Mum. It'll just be different.

We are sat in the living room with the morning light coming through the small cottage windows and all the lamps are on in the corners of the room and she says, David, can you turn the big light on?

I hate the big light. It makes the room feel even more dingy and a fly always seems to get in and go round and round and round the lampshade.

It's light enough, Mum.

Did you say tea?

Yes.

Yes, please then, she says.

I get up from the chair beside her, flick the big light on, which does nothing for anyone's eyesight, and make her a cup of tea in the kitchen. I do her some toast on the grill and lather it up with butter and marmalade.

Your nan loved the May Day celebrations, dear of her. She'd be up before dawn dressing the house. Whistling the Flora Day tune, Mum says.

That's where you get it from I expect, Mum.

Yes, I 'speck so. Comes around quick.

I let her gaze into the pictures without saying a word, and her toast cools on the table until all the butter has run through the bread.

Come on, let's drink these outside.

Okay. Where's Tony? she says, and I shrug. Where's your father? she says again.

Not sure. Maybe out the front? I think he was feeding his roses before dressing the house.

He better get a wriggle on, she says. Won't be long.

We walk slowly into the small back garden where she tends her sweet peas, which she has sown into every available bit of earth. Like the family photos, she has to work with the earth and seed close to her face.

A young boy runs down Garret Street with a cornet in his hand. I can just about hear the band warming up on the harbour, minus a young cornet player.

I hold Mum's arm and her tea in the other hand, and we stop and look at each pot and I explain what is happening. Not much here. Mum, I say. Small shoots in this one, Mum. I want to lie and say there is a cacophony of colours in her terracotta pot, but I don't because she'll know I'm having her on. She can smell a sweet pea in her garden from the chapel up on the headland.

Do you remember last year's spring? Now that was a good year.

I do remember, I tell her.

Last year the colours blurred to pastel smudges of red, purple and white, and passers-by would stop and smell them. You could smell them before you saw them, to be fair. They'd waft down the streets of Kingsand like a spreading fire. People would lean over our back wall and watch her pick them and tie them off and ask her what her secret is. Sea air, she'd say. And the seaweed from Cawsand. Only time I ever go to Cawsand! For their seaweed. Dunno why, but 'tis bleddy good stuff.

Tell them about your mother, my dad would say, whilst raking manure into his roses.

They don't want to hear about she, Mum would reply, embarrassed by the false theatre that Dad was setting up.

Oh, we do! the passers-by would say.

See, they do, Father would say.

Well, Mother lived here in this cottage for ninety-seven years and she only went around that bend once. She'd point to big grey cottage on the end of Market Street.

What's round that bend? visitors would ask.

The river runs under there, see. 'Tis the end of Kingsand and the start of Porthbugh.

Porthbugh?

Cawsand. Cow harbour, I'd say.

Might as well have been the end of the world for Mother, Porthbugh.

Why did she go around the corner only once?

Seaweed, of course.

I know it wasn't for seaweed. Mum told me that Gran had dashed round that bend Christmas Eve night 1977 to fetch the doctor from the Cross Keys, who was drinking whisky at the bar and playing darts with the fisherman. Grandad had a heart attack. By the time they got back, he was gone. No wonder she never went around that bend again.

The church strikes ten and the band bursts into song. The first dancers will be dancing round the May Pole, and I say to Mum, Shall we walk down and watch the children dance?

No, she says. I want to stay here and wait for the Black Prince.

OK, I say. I'll pop some seats out in a minute.

The sweet peas are sprouting everywhere. They are sprouting in the cracks of the path. In between the small patio slabs. By the wall. By the door. By the drain. Seeds that she has dropped and have germinated in the tiniest of places.

The bamboo canes are in place in the pots and are ready to hold the green shoots when the time comes. I place her hand on the canes and she makes sure they're tied together tightly, lacing her fingers around the bamboo and the string. She feels the height of them and taps the top, rubbing her thumb over the cane in circles. Mind your eyes on these, David, she says. Just at the right height to catch you.

Shall we cut some spring flowers for tomorrow? I ask her.

Yes, she says, and secateurs appear from her apron pocket, and she kneels at her pots. There are peonies and irises, and she holds them between her fingers. They'll look lovely and fresh, and we can throw them on to the Black Prince when it passes, she says.

Sarah? Sarah? It's Dad, calling from the front door through the house.

Yes?

Can you come around the front and help me?

His failings are her fault. It's always been this way. She is liable. She must help. She is the help. By the time I've taken a deep breath and stepped outside the front door, Dad is a few feet up a ladder and Mum has her foot on the second rung, her skirt over her knee. It frightens me how quickly she moves for him when instructed.

He's tying the Clematis Montana off to an upstairs window. He's fixed some screws into the red brickwork to help him tie shrubbery securely.

I can see the Black Prince coming down Fore Street. They're quite far away, but they're moving quickly.

Pass me the secateurs, he barks.

People have gathered right outside our house, and they turn to look at the sharpness of his tone. It's like the secateurs have cut right through them before they look back up Fore Street. The drums are building and the singing echoes through the tiny streets.

She puts her hand into a pocket. They're not there.

I'll get them, Mum. They're round the back. On the pot.

Hello, David. A voice from the gate. It's Martin, an old school friend of mine that moved away for university and never came back.

No, don't go, keep your foot on the bloody ladder woman!

How are you?

I'm well, thank you. I just need to …

Still living in the old village then?

Uh …

Okay, now go. I'm secure.

Are you sure?

Yes! I'm fine here.

… Yes. I've not gone far.

I watch Mum feel along the wall and step into the dark coolness of the house. Dad turns and sees the parade that is already halfway down Fore Street.

Why would you want to? says Martin. It's so beautiful here. I never saw it really. You know, when I lived here.

Mum! I yell. Yes, true. Gotta keep an eye on the old place. How about you?

The drums, the singing, the laughing are getting louder.

Martin is talking about law and London and commuting and his parents, and he takes his mobile phone out of his pocket and flicks the camera open. He takes a picture looking up Fore Street.

Mum! I shout. Mum!

Martin smiles at me. You haven't changed a bit, he says.

Dad is descending the ladder when Martin calls out to him. Hello, Mr Thomas. Martin Rescorla! I remember you coming on a school trip to help out when we were seven or eight.

Dad stops halfway down and twists to see who is talking to him. Oh yes! You went to school with David, didn't you? Didn't he, David?

Yes, Dad. The ladder wobbles. Put your foot on the ladder, Dad says.

Your roses are looking fabulous this year, Mr Thomas.

Ah thank you, Martin. Hoping for a bumper few wins at the village show this year with them. The winter has been mild, which has done them well. He steps off the ladder and shakes hands with Martin.

What sort of roses are they? Martin asks, but then I see it, the Black Prince on the shoulders of four Navy cadets in their immaculate uniforms, beaming with pride and ale and rum. They're passing the entrance to the car park and people stand on walls and children are on fathers' shoulders to see the Black Prince twist and turn.

And then they're outside our house and people dance and jig and Martin films on his phone.

Mum! I shout.

Stop yelling, David. She's coming. Dad raises his voice over the frivolities.

Except she doesn't have time, and the boat sails by on those broad shoulders of those Navy men without her flowers being cast upon them.

The crowds follow. Martin follows and suggests a pint later and mentions a school reunion I know nothing about that is planned for September.

Mum is stood in the doorframe with the secateurs in one hand and spring flowers in the other. She steps carefully down the steps and reaches out for my hand. As she reaches for me, she drops the flowers on the path.

I've missed it, haven't I? she says, tears in her eyes.

We'll catch it up, I say. Come on, we can catch them.

Pass me the secateurs, will you? says Dad, who is back up the ladder and has begun tying off a couple of loose ends. I want to follow the Prince down to the harbour and see it off.

But she doesn't hand them to him.

She stumbles to his roses.

Sarah, what are you doing? Again, he twists on the ladder to shout at her.

She takes a rose between her thumb and forefinger and gently rubs her thumb over the petals.

Snip.

She cuts the rose with as much stem as possible.

Dad makes an indistinguishable noise that is somewhere between pain and shock. It's as if he has jumped in the sea on the hottest day of the year and the cold water has taken his breath away.

Snip.

Snip.

He's clambering down the ladder, which is shaking. In fact, he is shaking.

Snip.

Snip.

Sarah! For goodness' sake, what are you doing woman?

I grab his arm and stop him in his tracks. He tries to shake me off like a crab, but my clench is too firm.

Snip.

Snip. Snip.

Mum finishes cutting the roses and turns to the gate.

She strides confidently across the garden and opens the gate and takes one step outside onto the pavement. She leans back and, with all her might, throws the roses down Fore Street. The wind catches them, and they immediately scatter over the road and the pavement amongst the other spring flowers and plastic pint glasses that have been scattered and discarded.

Come on, she says to me, and I let go of Dad's arm. Mum is halfway down Garrett Street trailing her hand along the wall when I catch her up.

In a hurry? I say to her.

I want to see if the Black Prince sails or sinks.

Course you do, I say.

You'll have to tell me.

I will, Mum. Don't worry.

She holds my hand, and she stops briefly by the village

hall and says, I didn't eat the toast you did me.

Ah well.

Yeah. Never mind. Your Dad will eat it.

I place her hand on the canes and she makes sure they're tied together tightly, lacing her fingers around the bamboo and the string.

AUTHOR

Edward Rowe

Rame Peninsula, they call you 'the forgotten corner of Cornwall', because a fair few holidaymakers seem to bypass you and head to Newquay, St Ives and beyond. Thirty-seven miles from Roche, fifty miles from Truro and a whopping eighty-six miles from Land's End. I don't think people in Cornwall have forgotten you, I think it's just a bit of a drive. And because it's a bit of a drive, you are the part of Cornwall I still know least well – which makes you very special to me. I can visit for an afternoon in May and pick up fish 'n' chips, sit and watch the Torpoint Ferry go back and forth and feel like I'm on holiday. The narrow streets of Kingsand Cawsand, the giant warships offshore steaming back into Plymouth, the tranquillity of St John and Millbrook and Seaton that seems to be gradually disappearing throughout the rest of Cornwall – it's familiar, but never familiar enough, and I really like that feeling. I won't forget you Rame Peninsula, I promise.

THE MONKEY IN

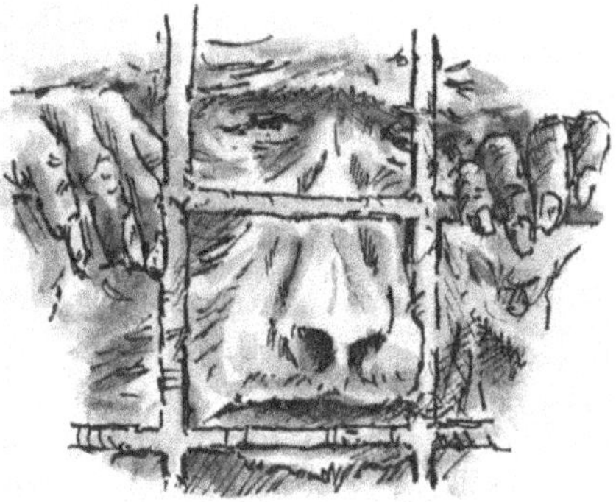

THE WOODSHED

by Luke Thompson
(Section 12 Bodmin Moor)

'Do you like animals,' said the old man, his cottongrass brows pressing down over murky eyes, obscuring them like mist over a marsh pool. 'I have a monkey in the woodshed. Would you like to see?'

Two competing thoughts went through Jack Cormorant's head when he was asked if he wanted to see the old man's monkey. The first was something like, That sentence is straight from a horror movie, the kind where the young man gets murdered in the woodshed and fed to a monkey that may or may not be real. The second thought was, If I say 'No', I will forever regret the story I might have been able to tell about the scary old man in the mire and his monkey.

'Well?' said the old man.

'Lead on,' said Jack.

If the monkey in the woodshed were the strangest thing about this farm on the moor Jack might have been fine.

It was meant to be romantic and spontaneous, driving down to Trewortha to see Ysella, but the snow had forced the traffic on the A30 into a single-track over the moors. Jack was still feeling bold and spontaneous as he crawled down the dual carriageway, the snowfall driving in towards the windshield, flashing and disorienting in the headlights. It was when he turned off to Trewortha and the road had not been cleared and the snow was so thick he could scarcely tell where the verge was and his leg began to tremble as it hovered over the pedals, afeared to touch any of them for risk of sliding – it was then that the bladder of romance and heroism was emptied.

In just a few minutes Jack had driven away from civilisation and into the wilderness of the night and the moors. He slid the car along the narrow road for a short time but the snow meant he could hardly see, and the stone cross that marked the turning onto the higher moor seemed to arrive quite suddenly. Instinctively he tapped the brake, realising the mistake immediately. The car slid and Jack could do nothing but wait for the impact. The granite cross thumped into the corner of the bonnet. The airbag went off impotently, scorching Jack's shirtsleeve, and the smell of the wrecked engine and the burning cloth filled the car.

'Shit,' said Jack, fingering the burn on his arm, which he knew would start to hurt before long. He opened the door and the cold blasted him. He could no longer hear the main road or see its lights. He reached for his phone. 'Shit,' he repeated. Ysella had warned him there was no reception. She used to drive up over North Hill to call him.

'Now what?' he asked himself. Well he couldn't sit here all night. There was no sign on the road of any other vehicles having passed through the snow, the car was buggered, and the cold would be overwhelming before long. He wondered how far he was from Trewortha. It couldn't be that far. Perhaps he should carry on by foot. At any rate, he was bound to come across a house before long.

When he stepped out of the car it was perfect darkness. He put on his coat and tightened his boots. His phone had enough battery for the torch to work a while, for what that was worth.

He took off down the lane, the hedges in the dissipated phone light guiding him for his first few steps. Within fifty yards Jack fell. The hedge had ended with a cattle grid, covered over by the snowfall, and Jack got his leg trapped and hit his forearm so hard his hand went numb. Slowly he pulled himself out. His shin was throbbing, grazed and bleeding beneath his trousers. But he didn't stop.

Beyond the cattle grid the landscape changed quite suddenly to open moor. There must be a road but Jack would be damned if he could tell where it was. He wished there was someone to tell him which direction to go in.

In the dim light he could make out what seemed to be a contour – the dip of a path, he thought – and … What was that? A light? In the falling snow it flickered in and out of sight, a dim blue emanation. 'Thank God,' he said out loud, and without hesitation struck out towards it. Almost immediately his foot fell through the snow and into the marsh. It poured over his boot and the black mud beneath tried to keep hold. The marsh gulped as it let go.

Now where was that light? Was that it? No. Yes. He tripped on a tussock, slipped back, fell again. His phone extinguished in the water.

'Shit!' he shouted. 'I give up.'

He stood again, soaked through, turned. Which way was the car? There was no moon. His eyes were night-blind. The blue light! There it was again. Well if the blue light is ahead of me then I just need to turn back the opposite way, Jack reasoned. He felt the ground give with every step. Softer, wetter, grabbing. Time and again he fell. He was shivering painfully, his hands pulsating from the cold and the falls. There was the blue light. How could it be coming closer? Jack did not like it. He tried to move more swiftly, but now he was sure he had taken a bad turn. Then the ground gave altogether. He fell forward, his head hit moorstone and his body began to sink slowly into the marsh.

Next thing he recalled was something grabbing at his

arm. He wrenched away, thinking it was some moorland beast or eel, but it held him and would not let go, gripping his forearm like a crab squeezing a mussel. It hauled him from the marsh with incredible strength, tugging on that arm as though trying to tear it from his body. It pulled him into a shallower pool and he lay with his head on a sphagnum-soft hummock.

'You dead?' a voice said. A toe was prodding him in the ribs.

Jack raised his head. A broad figure stood over him, a great square head and beard, wearing a broad-brimmed hat and stinking wax coat that dragged in the marsh. The figure was holding a lantern so close to his face he could feel the heat. It looked like something from two centuries before but burned with a bluish light.

'Not dead,' said the figure. 'Up then.'

Jack was hauled to his feet. He staggered and splashed in the marsh.

'Huh,' grunted the figure and turned his back on the boy. The bright blue light had made Jack night-blind again so he kept close to the oily shadow who was confidently striding off. Striding deeper into the marsh and never faltering, never sinking, never stumbling.

'Where are we going?'

'Home.'

The house was slate hung, shadow-black in the snowlight, except for large orbs of brilliant white – lumps of quartz from the clitters and quarries, no doubt

– decorating the face. As they got closer, and the light of the lamp and the windows illuminated the farm more starkly, Jack saw they were not lumps of quartz but … skulls. Row upon row of skulls, presumably claimed from the marsh just as Jack had been claimed. Horse skulls and sheep skulls and … no, it couldn't be.

'Not dead', said the figure.'Up then.'

'Take off your clothes,' said the old man as he closed the door behind them.

'I can't.'

'You're not coming in like that.'

'I have to see Ysella.'

'Eh?'

'I'm on my way to Ysella at Trewortha.'

The old man looked at the boy standing in the hallway, soaked through with peaty marsh water, a gob of moss snagged on the lace of a boot. 'Lucky girl,' he said.

Inside the squat farmhouse, the air was thick with acrid blue-grey smoke and the light in the hallway was dim. The queer old moor man took off his long coat and wide-brimmed hat and it was only now, his features softened by the fog of the fire, that Jack caught a glimpse of him, large and thick set, a worn woollen suit the colour of larks and hair white as kaolinite.

He left Jack in the hall shivering and dripping onto the slate floor and stomped up the wide wooden stairs, each foot falling as though stamping in a nail. Jack heard a key turning with a series of heavy clicks. A door groaned and shuddered. More stomping. Another door, a gentle creak, the sounds growing fainter. He heard the old man grumbling.

Jack had been staring at the stairs all the while, as though mesmerised. He was shaking uncontrollably. For a moment he thought of leaving, but he knew he couldn't make his way through the marsh and the snow and the night. He imagined his own skull hanging on the wall outside.

When the old man returned he was carrying a black bundle. He stomped back down the stairs and threw it at the pathetic young man who had not moved an inch since he left. The bundle fell at his feet.

'You shiver so hard you're rattling the roof slates,' said the old man. 'Take your clothes off. Put these on. Bathroom through there.' The old man turned away and wandered through the smoke to the far end of the room, where there was a small heavy door, which he stooped through, closing it behind him. The smoke churned in his wake.

At Jack's feet was a faded suit. He took the bundle to the bathroom. The suit was too lean to have been the old man's but it just about fitted Jack, with some six inches of extra leg and sleeve flapping at the extremities. He was still shivering as he descended into the caliginous dining room, bare feet timid on the cold floor. As his eyes adjusted to the gloom he saw the dim light beneath the heavy door. He padded over the slates and fur rug. How did that man even fit through this door, he thought. Even he had to stoop. He pushed it open as quietly as he could.

The old man was sitting in front of a fire, black lumps of turf heaped up, smouldering. Smoke was coming back down the chimney, as though the wind was in the wrong direction or the chimney blocked. Around the edge of the room were shelves of books and pickle jars. It was too murky to see what was in them. Between them, in unfashionable oval frames, were smoke-jaundiced watercolours of wildflowers – tormentil, sundew, lousewort.

The old man was pouring himself wine from a milk bottle when he heard the young man and turned in his armchair.

'Where are your clothes?'

'I left them in the bathroom.'

'You want them dry?'

'Well, yes.'

'Not so dry in the bathroom.'

'I didn't want to get the floor wet.'

'Stone floor.'

'Still…'

'Hmph.'

'I'll fetch them, shall I?'

They sat in front of the fire, chuffs of smoke pulsing back down and out into the world while Jack's clothes steamed like a piskie-ridden pony. He stared into the turf.

'Wine?'

'Well I won't be driving again tonight.'

'Hmph.'

There wasn't much left in the bottle after he'd poured. The old man rose and left the room. Jack listened again. The turf burned silently and Jack could hear the old man padding through the dining room. He heard a splashing sound – footsteps walking through water – a pause, then the footsteps returning. The old man's slippers were dripping when he came back.

'Where did you go?' asked Jack.

'Kitchen.'

'But your feet.'

'Floor's wet.'

'I guessed that.'

The old man didn't say anything for a while. Then he gave a slightly startled 'Hmph!' A tiny green frog was clambering through his furzy beard. He almost seemed to smile, the storm cloud of his countenance dissipating.

'Must have picked him up in the kitchen,' said the old man. The frog struggled up towards the old man's mouth but got tangled, then, clumsily extricating its feet from a grey curl, it fell onto the old man's knee, leapt to the floor and bounced away. 'Lots of frogs.'

'What, in your kitchen?'

'Good marsh,' he said. The cloud began to thicken again, then the old man roused himself. 'Look.' He pointed at a shelf, rose and reached behind the pickle jars, pulling out what looked like jerked meat – a stiff lump of black flesh – which he dropped in Jack's lap.

'Oh shit!' cried Jack.

'Bog toad. Preserved. Like a mummy. I have newts too.'

'That's disgusting.'

'Hmph.'

'Hold on,' said Jack. 'What's in the jars?'

'Things I've found. Things I've caught. Some decayed above ground. Bones and skins. Belong to the mire, see. She's a slow eater.' The old man filled the wine glasses and sat back down. 'Important to stay topped up.'

'You took these from the marsh?'

'Took?' said the old man. 'We're still in the marsh.'

'I mean …' It didn't matter. Jack was beginning to feel drowsy.

'Always emptying, always filling,' said the old man.

Jack placed the bog toad on the arm of his chair. The wine and the turf fire were making his skin tingle and his eyes heavy. The old man glanced at him and looked away again. Jack noticed the look and didn't like it. He tried to waken himself. He thought of Ysella.

'I should go,' he said. 'I can't stay here all night.'

'All night,' echoed the old man.

'I have to get to Trewortha.'

'Yes.'

'Which way gets me out of here?'

'None tonight.'

'There must be a way out.'

'You won't find one.'

'Do you know a way?'

'I'm not going out in this snow.'

'You came to find me.'

The old man didn't answer.

'Do you have a torch I could borrow?' Jack tried. 'I think I could make it with a torch.'

'I need my lamp. Don't want you losing it in the marsh.'

'If I had a torch I wouldn't lose anything!'

'You don't know the marsh.'

'Well I'm going anyway.'

'You're warm, aren't you?' said the old man. 'Stay with me.'

'Why won't you help me?'

The old man didn't say anything. He got to his feet and left the room. Jack heard him walking across the stone floor. Then he heard the jangling of heavy keys followed by the grinding noise of a lock being turned and the sharp hammer of an iron bolt. He heard the sound of splashing again – footsteps in the kitchen – and Jack ran out of the room to check the front door. It was locked and the key had gone.

'Shit,' he said, and then he heard the splashing again. Before he could dash back to the hearth the old man was back in the room.

'I should call the police,' said Jack.

'Why?'

'My car,' said Jack, but he was not thinking of his car. 'It's on the road. I lost control and hit a stone cross.'

'A cross?'

'May I use the phone?'

'Go on,' said the old man and wandered back through the smoke to the turf fire.

'Right.'

Jack looked around. He went to the top of the stairs and tried the doors, fumbling through the darkness. They were all locked. He returned to the hall, stood in silence, then went back, defeated, to the acrid room with the faded watercolours and pickled beasts where the old man had poured himself another glass of wine.

'Where's your phone?' said Jack.

'What phone?'

'You said I could use your phone.'

'Hmph.' The old man took a gulp of wine and cleared his throat. And that's when he asked, 'Do you like animals?'

'Here, put these on.' The old man handed him a pair of battered boots. They were covered with holes and incredibly heavy.

'Geez!' said Jack.

'Steel toes.'

'Oh.'

'Heavy rubber.'

'Will I need them?'

'He bites.'

'Can he jump?'

'Yes he can,' said the old man with the slightest of smiles in his eyes, something like pride. 'He jumps well.'

'Well what if he jumps? Couldn't he bite me in the throat?'

'He could, he could. He jumps well,' said the old man. 'He could jump right over your head, I'd say.'

'Then what good are the boots?'

'If he bites you in the throat?'

'Yes!'

'Well, they'd be no good at all.'

He held up his lamp and led Jack through the kitchen, the floor a wetland of sphagnum and black water. Now and then something would trouble the surface.

'Was that an eel?' said Jack as a long dark body snapped and writhed.

The old man didn't answer.

The woodshed had a stack of turf outside with a weighted thatch protecting it from the weather. Tonight the thatch was thick with snow. The old man unlatched the door and stepped inside, his lamp illuminating the room. Jack couldn't see anything to begin with, save for a scruffy woodpile and a second mouldy turf stack, but he sensed something shuffling in the dark. Two glinting eyes in the shadow. It was a big monkey!

The creature did not move, but as Jack's eyes got used to the darkness he began to make out a little more of its strange form.

'Are you sure it's a monkey?'

'It's a baboon.'

It didn't look like a baboon to Jack.

'What kind of baboon?'

'Monkey expert, are you?'

'No, I just …'

'Huh.'

'Are you?'

'I know baboons.'

'You know baboons,' Jack repeated. 'It just doesn't look like any baboon I've seen before.'

'Quite something.'

'What does it do in here?' Jack looked around the woodshed, his eye catching something on the floor. 'Is that a book?'

'Hymns Ancient and Modern.'

'The monkey reads?' Jack joked.

The cottongrass brows pressed into a scowl. 'Sings.'

Jack began to wonder a little more urgently whether his clothes were dry yet.

'Look,' said the old man, pulling a handbell from his pocket, as though to distract Jack. The monkey's eyes followed the old man's movements carefully. 'It loves the bell. Go on.' He handed Jack the bell.

Jack shook it with the vigour of the damned. The sound filled the barn in an unnatural way and the baboon tensed. Jack rang it again and the creature leapt forward baring its teeth. Jack cried out and fell back, scrambling away until he was pressed against the barn wall. The bell dropped to the floor and the baboon grabbed it and retreated to the shadows.

'I have to leave,' said Jack. 'I have to go.'

'It loves that bell.'

'Right now. I'm going.'

'You haven't heard it sing yet.'

'Baboons don't sing. I'm getting my coat.' Jack flung open the shed door and dashed out into the cold back towards the house. He splashed through the kitchen and picked up his coat. The old man had followed him slowly. Jack heard him lock the back door behind him.

'I have to go,' Jack repeated, almost in tears.

'But I don't have a pickle jar big enough for you if you go out there.'

Jack pulled at the door. He knew it was locked but there was nothing else he could do.

'Once you leave,' continued the old man, 'you can't come back. I'll lock this door and that's that.'

'Open the door. Let me out.'

'You're wearing my wellies.'

'I don't care.'

'They'll wash clean, I suppose.'

'Open the door!'

The old man smiled, reached into his waistcoat pocket and pulled out an iron key. He turned it in the lock, wiggled the bolt loose from the bolthole and opened the door. Smoke poured out into the night and across the mire.

Jack dashed outside. The snow had stopped, but it was bitterly cold. He stood in front of the house, turned to look back. In the light from the doorway he could see the skulls glowing against the black slate and the silhouette of the giant old man. He was shutting the door. Locking it. Bolting it. For just a moment the skulls remained illuminated, leering down, grimacing, before they, with the house, like some fairy dance, seemed to vanish into the shadow of the mire. There was a sound. Was it bells? The gentlest of breezes seemed to carry the sound. Church bells? And closer, faintly, a reedy organ, and a voice.

A broad figure stood over him, a great square head and beard, wearing a broad-brimmed hat and stinking wax coat that dragged in the marsh.

AUTHOR

Luke Thompson

East Moor has everything. Every kind of history. There's literary history here, with Sabine Baring-Gould almost drowning in the Redmoor Marsh and Daphne du Maurier losing her way on an excursion from the Jamaica Inn. There's natural history, from the carnivorous sundews and the beautiful bog cotton to the lapwings and abundant cuckoos. And there's the longer kind of history too. Bodmin Moor has the whole of Cornwall condensed into just a few square miles, and nowhere more so than East Moor, with Bronze Age cairns, a stone circle, medieval settlements and field systems, mining, quarrying, farming, peat-cutting and timber plantations - it's got everything. I used to live just below East Moor and spent a lot of time up here, long afternoons walking and longer nights sleeping under a stunted hawthorn in the ruins of what I believe was a medieval hut or grave.

Author photograph: Ellie Hope

EDITORS NOTES

Winter. A row of legs, immersed up to the knees in a trench of icy, liquid mud. Picks and shovels strike an unstable wall of earth. Men's wearied faces display a determination to uncover the lodes of precious ore hidden within, the fear of being buried alive should the wall collapse and the strain of standing, feet mired, for hours at a time, day after day, persistently wielding their tools.

This series of extreme closeups, interspersed with wide-angle shots of the landscape, all in black and white (think one of Italian auteur Sergio Leone's spaghetti westerns meets Cornish writer-director Mark Jenkin's BAFTA-winning film Bait) provided the inspiration for this anthology.

Back in September 2021, I was invited by Cornwall National Landscape to run a series of creative writing workshops for their Bodmin Environment Arts Science and Theatre (BEAST) event, held beside Colliford Lake, Cornwall's largest reservoir, on Bodmin Moor.

Before one of the workshops, local author and tour guide Mark Camp treated the participants and me to a walking tour, to get the proverbial creative juices flowing. Or, in my case, the internal 16mm Bolex whirring. It was during this tour that Mark talked about the tin streaming that had taken place on the valley bottom in Medieval times. First came the opening scenes of my mental masterpiece, and nipping at its heels came the idea for an anthology of short stories inspired by the twelve sections of the Cornwall National Landscape, each written by a different Cornwall-based writer.

I pitched this idea to Melodie Manners at Cornwall National Landscape, who had invited me to run the BEAST workshops. Melodie was enthusiastic, and within a few days had secured funding. I swung my pick and hit a rich vein of ore straight away. As anybody who's ever tried to get a creative project like this off the ground, and likely also those Medieval labourers, would tell you, this sort of thing never happens.

Out there, in the big wide world, or 'up north' as anybody who's lived in Cornwall for more than a few weeks would say, people like Melodie are rare. But not here. Not in Cornwall. And especially not in the writing community, which is defined by the enthusiasm, generosity of spirit and openness of its people.

It was Amanda Harris, then Director of The Writers' Block, the Cornish writing centre, based in Redruth, where I've run workshops for several years, who recommended me to Cornwall National Landscape.

It was also Amanda who told me about Hermitage Press, a new independent publisher committed to publishing the work of Cornwall-based writers. And as soon as Melodie gave the anthology the green light, I contacted Dr Paul Taylor-McCartney the original CEO of Hermitage Press to see if he'd be interested in considering it for publication. He was. Not only that, he offered his support throughout the process of putting the anthology together, before he'd seen a word, or even the names of the contributors, let alone agreed to publish it. Paul, like Amanda, and Hermitage's new CEO, Sam Stone, cares deeply about Cornwall and its writers.

The same goes for all the writers in this anthology. Our budget wasn't huge, yet I managed to persuade some of Cornwall's foremost talents, such as Cathy Rentzenbrink, Philip Marsden and Wyl Menmuir, to contribute, as well as actor-director-writer Edward Rowe (AKA Kernow King), star of the aforementioned Bait. Actually, no persuasion was required. Within days, and without a question, they all said, *'Yes'.* As did everybody else I asked. Every writer who has contributed to this anthology was on the A-list of names I produced before Melodie even commissioned it. It's a potent blend of some of Cornwall's most established literary practitioners and most talented emerging writers. And, in my (apparently not so) humble opinion, it's produced magic.

For me, the Cornish landscape, like the landscape of my native Wales, contains all the yesterdays that have unfolded in it. All the lives lived. All the stories. And it doesn't take much for it to start speaking to me, for the past to come to life in my head. Cornwall is a place of spectacular natural beauty (exemplified by the fact it's the only National Landscape in the United Kingdom with twelve distinct sections. It's also a place where community and connection, both to people and place, matter. And there's no better way to connect than through stories.

Cornish culture is rich with folklore, legend, myth, spirituality and the supernatural. All of these things combined make it a place that people leave but can never forget and long to return to. It seeps into your bones.

Not wanting to restrict each writer's craft or imagination, I didn't provide an overly detailed brief, but – unless it's universal, which is quite possible – I must have conveyed what the Cornish landscape means to me, because the twelve stories in this anthology encapsulate it.

All of the stories also capture something of the image of medieval tin workers that originally inspired them. Some have a contemporary setting, some have a historical setting and some span generations – but they're all deeply rooted in both the Cornish landscape and human experience. Most of them are 'dark'. All of them will make you think and, most importantly, make you feel.

Perhaps one day Mark Jenkin will adapt them into a series of short films, all starring Edward Rowe, of course. For now, you have the words on the pages, accompanied by James Innerdale's beautiful illustrations. You have the twelve most outstandingly beautiful sections of the Cornish landscape. And that should be enough for anybody.

I hope you enjoy reading *Twelve Stories for Twelve Sections* as much as I enjoyed my part in creating it.

With thanks, *Gareth Rees*

OUR ILLUSTRATOR

James Innerdale

The landscape of Cornwall can be beautiful, inspiring, but at times dark and threatening and intertwined are stories and tales that reflect its many moods. As an illustrator it was both a pleasure and a challenge to weave these various strands into the accompanying illustrations for the new Twelve Stories for Twelve Sections anthology. I have attempted to create fresh images to reflect the contemporary yet timeless quality of the stories, whilst allowing plenty of room for the imagination.

THANK YOU TO OUR GUIDES

Connecting people with the Cornwall National Landscape is, in part, made possible by the relationships that we've built with a cohort of expert guides out in the 12 Areas of Outstanding Natural Beauty sections. These individuals are passionate advocates for the protected landscape in Cornwall, and the knowledge they possess about the places they live and work is unparalleled.

It's been such a pleasure to be able to introduce them to the authors in this anthology. Eager to share their considerable knowledge, they have generously given their time to support this project – and it's much appreciated. Versed in the nuances of Cornwall's cultural heritage, as well as the shifting character of the landscape, in the way only lived experience brings, they have brought depth to the sense of place that flows through the stories in the anthology.

I would like to thank these expert guides, who have taken our authors under their wings and shown them aspects of the 12 sections that might otherwise have gone unseen. Jon Stewart from North Cornwall National Trust, who imparted the rich history of Section 02 to Jane Pugh; Hugh St Aubyn who illuminated the mystical heritage of St Michael's Mount for Cathy Rentzenbrink; Nick Taylor, who wowed C.M. Davis with the intricacies of the Cornish Hedge in West Penwith; Adrian Langdon, who brought the Camel Estuary to life beyond the Camel Trail for Polly Roberts; Dick Cole, who helped Emma Timpany celebrate the life of Cornwall's patron saint; and Mark Camp, whose knowledge of the legends of North and East Cornwall knows no bounds and informed the stories by Edward Rowe and Wyl Menmuir.

A sense of place is intangible; the task of putting it into words was not an insignificant ask – so thank you.

Melodie Manners
Business Development Officer